Summer, 1758. All around the woods of Fort Ticonderoga, silence. The crazing sound of the bagpipes had ceased and the air was electrified. An assault was about to begin against the strategic French fortress. Now the British Redcoats and their Mohawk allies were sliding through the trees noiselessly, filling the woods. Within the stronghold the French and the Hurons knew they were outnumbered by the enemy five to one.

But one young Indian did not choose sides. This was Fawn, the son of a French Jesuit and the grandson of a Mohawk warrior. He belonged to no group, followed no conventions, allied himself with no colonists. He knew that the soil for which the French and the British slaughtered each other was not theirs, but his. It was American.

ROBERT NEWTON PECK, a native son of Vermont, was born within a musket shot of Fort Ticonderoga. He now lives in Darien, Connecticut, with his wife and children. His other books include *Path of Hunters, Soup,* and, available from Dell, *Millie's Boy* and *A Day No Pigs Would Die.*

THE LAUREL-LEAF LIBRARY brings together under a single imprint outstanding works of fiction and nonfiction particularly suitable for young adult readers, both in and out of the classroom. The series is under the editorship of Charles F. Reasoner, Professor of Elementary Education, New York University.

FAWN

Robert Newton Peck

Published by
Dell Publishing Co., Inc.
1 Dag Hammarskjold Plaza
New York, New York 10017

Laurel-Leaf Library ® TM 766734,
Dell Publishing Co., Inc.

ISBN: 0-440-92488-X

Reprinted by arrangement with
Little, Brown and Company (Inc.)
Printed in the United States of America
First Laurel-Leaf printing—April 1977
Second Laurel-Leaf printing—June 1977
Third Laurel-Leaf printing—October 1978

Ticonderoga . . .

To the Black Watch who bled there.
To the Mohawk who starved there.
To the old man who saw me skin the rabbit.

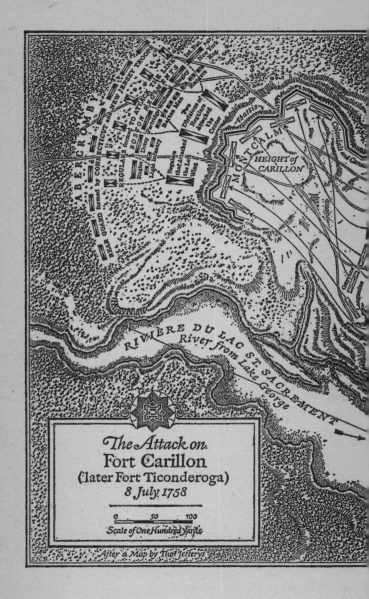

The Attack on
Fort Carillon
(later Fort Ticonderoga)
8 July 1758

0   50   100

Scale of One Hundred Yards

After a Map by Thos Jefferys

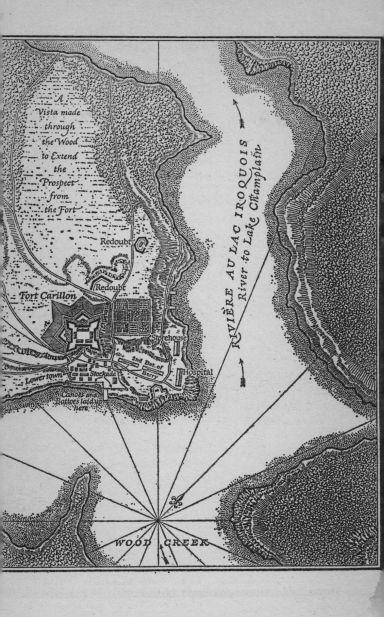

Fort Ticonderoga

Where the angry white water of Ticonderoga Creek cools to blue and silently slides among a stand of cattails, a fort was built by the French in 1755.

They named it Fort Carillon.

Four years hence, it was captured by a British force commanded by the able General Amherst and renamed Fort Ticonderoga. And when the slumbering English underestimated a tough troop of Vermont farmers who bore little more than squirrel rifles, the fort became American.

As within every child there is a toy soldier, few experiences will excite your military spirit as will an assault on today's Fort Ticonderoga. Stone by stone (using much of the original rock) the great gray star was remade according to the early blueprints of the French engineers. Today it stands as a breathtaking work of military masonry. You may patrol the high-wall ramparts, where children now straddle the cold barrels of massive cannon that could once bully Lake Champlain. And in the dark explore the dungeon.

Gone is the sound of bugles. But beyond your inner ear, harken to a roll of drums, a ghostly paradiddle by a freckled drummer boy long dead. Or hear a haunted sting of Scottish bagpipes.

As you retreat, Old Glory battles the wind, high above the stubborn stone, to honor the memory of brave men, both red and white, who fought and fell where you now walk free along a path of history.

Stories of Ticonderoga are many. Our story begins

in 1741 in a Huron canoe paddled south from Canada.
Leaving the lower lake, which had been discovered
by Samuel de Champlain more than a century earlier,
two men portaged the canoe up along the steep trail,
to avoid the white falls of LaChute, to the upper lake.
One man was red, the other white.

The red man was naked in the summer sun, a Huron from the north whose name is not in our story.
The white man was Henri Charbon, a Frenchman
born in France but now a Jesuit, a priest in a long
black robe.

Even before the two rested their canoe at the water's edge of the upper lake, the red man grunted that
he wished to go no farther. He made signs to his com-
panion that this was the land of the Mohawk, the slay-
ers. No place for a Jesuit or a Huron warrior. The
Frenchman made signs to his guide, asking him to be
still. But the Huron would not be silent, nor would he
continue south, where enemies would pull his skin
from his bones.

From among the silent trees came a hissing sound.
The Huron fell; a Mohawk arrow had passed through
his back, and its bloody triangular head protruded
from his belly. The Jesuit waited for the second arrow
to come. Holding his small black book, his breviary,
he prayed to his God . . . not to save him, only to die
bravely.

No second arrow came. And there was no sound
and no stir among the trees. Dipping his fingers into
the cool water, he placed his wet hand on the head of
his fallen guide.

"I baptize thee in the name of the Father, and the
Son," he said softly in Latin, "and in the Holy Spirit.
May thy soul . . ."

The Huron groaned, rolling over. He was still alive.
Henri could see that his eyes were open and wildly
searching.

Looking up quickly, the Jesuit saw a band of naked
red men curiously watching him. Were they the Iro-

quois, he thought, the allies of the British? His knees seemed to freeze to the hard ground and he could not rise. Was this how Jogues had felt, and all the tortured Jesuits who earlier had ventured south to the land of the Mohawk? I do not want to die. I must think quickly. What does one say to a savage?

"I am a man of God," he said in English, hoping they had heard enough of the language to comprehend, "and I come in peace. I carry no musket."

Slowly, one of the Mohawk warriors walked toward him. As he approached, Henri could not force himself to rise but remained on his knees. He could smell a strong animal smell. The Mohawk's face showed no understanding, no hatred, and even less compassion. Saying nothing, the warrior drew back his foot, and then gave the prone Huron's crotch a vicious kick. Bending over, he tore out the arrow, and then spat on the groaning Huron. Placing his foot on the man's head, he stepped down, grinding the man's face into the dirt. Behind him, the dozen other Mohawk warriors made grunting sounds of amusement.

As the Huron moaned in pain, the face of the Mohawk chief seemed to be pleased that the bleeding man was not yet dead. Both of us, Henri thought, will die slowly.

The Mohawk advanced to where Henri still knelt on the ground. Reaching forward, the red man lifted the black wide-brimmed hat from Henri's head and placed it upon his own. The other Mohawks made noises of appreciation. With his left hand, the Mohawk grabbed Henri's hair in his fist, yanking back his head. His right hand pressed the blood-dripping point of the arrow to the Jesuit's throat. Then he spoke, in English.

"Black Robe," he said.

"Yes," said Henri, "for I am a priest. I am called Father."

"I am called . . . Old Foot."

One

Fawn lay still.

The soft summer storm had passed over the lake, leaving blacker tree trunks and the tap of raindrops skipping from leaf to leaf. The rainsoaked ground pressed cool and wet against his naked chest. He was afraid to move even a finger, although a sharp edge of rock bit into a rib and forced him to narrow his breathing.

Through the green-lace leaves of the white birch tree that curled up from the shore of the lake and then bent its boughs down nearly to touch the water, Fawn studied the splashing of the young forkhorn. The buck was less than fifty steps away, unaware of the cold blue eyes that pursued his every wading step.

Caught in the silver shallows of the lake, a trout fought for its freedom, trying to escape to deep water. But the split hoofs of the deer struck down on the back of the fish once more, until the spine snapped and it could no longer swim. Only then did the white-tailed forkhorn dip his delicate nose into the lake to seize his meal of trout. Holding the fish in his teeth, the deer whipped it from side to side—as a dog would shake a snake, filling the air with circles of silver drops.

Fawn could have pulled back his hunting bow, which lay as tight to earth as he. But instead he waited, charmed by a deer who had trapped a fish. The young forkhorn held his trout high in the air, letting the cool lakewater pour down from his catch and into his mouth; a swallow of water flavored with trout. Lowering his head until the four points of his antlers almost pricked the water, the buck tossed his head up quickly and released his jaws, flipping the trout into the air. Rearing on hind legs, he lunged upward, his mouth snaring the dead fish as if such sport was no feat at all.

Now! Fawn bent his bow, prepared to bury a bolt of hickory in the deer's heart, which he knew was just behind the shoulder.

Old Foot had taught Fawn well. Many summers had passed since the old Mohawk warrior (the father of his mother) had made Fawn his first hunting bow from a long tough maple sapling before his small grandson had the arm to pull it. And each day his grandfather, Old Foot, had knelt with him, demanding that his left arm be straight and firm as iron, urging him to do what at last he could do—pull back the bowstring (that was made from dried, twisted, smoked deer gut) until it cut the tip of his nose. Blood had spurted from under the fingernails of Fawn's right hand. A few red drops had run onto his chin, yet he did not release the bowstring until Old Foot had nodded. The warm fire of pride washed clean the cold sting of pain.

Fawn waited, as Old Foot would have waited, for the right target for his kill. Only the first arrow would fly from his bow. Deer do not wait for the second.

Tight against the wet moss of the lakeshore, Fawn felt the drum of his heart as if it beat upon the earth itself. It was like this with every deer. For until today, every deer that Fawn had stalked had fled his arrows. But the taut gut of his bent bow pulled tighter, until Fawn could hear the wind strum the string into music, and the gut bit into his fingers, and sang . . . not this deer.

Fawn was now living his sixteenth summer, and he had not yet taken a deer. *This* deer, this young forkhorn, would be his first kill of venison. He must mark this day in his mind. The fifth day of July, 1758.

He released the arrow.

At the same moment, he saw the forkhorn spring high into the air and then fall on his side, all four of his legs violently kicking the growing circle of red water.

Fawn ran to the deer, cut the throat with his knife, drawing out his one true arrow that was now blood-red nearly back to its feathery wings.

Bringing the wet arrow to his lips (as he had seen Old Foot do) he tasted the strong warm blood of his deer. Lifting his eyes to look at the sky, he sang his quiet prayer of thanks to the God of all Mohawks and all people, asking Him to bless the kill. With the point of the hunting arrow he bloodied his own arm, covering the wound with a handful of wet dirt from the lake bottom. It was a tribute to the Earth Mother who spares life as often as She takes it away.

Nearby, the trout floated with its belly shining white in the late-afternoon sun, as dead as the deer. Looking down at the quivering tan body of the buck made the mist of sorrow fill Fawn's eyes. It was not manly, Old Foot had said, to cry; and he would never allow weeping for one's own hurt. But to share the hurt of others and to honor their death with tears was a good thing. Compassion was a gift of the Rabbit God, so that all men and all women would know moments alone in which to be shy and soft, and to cry without shame. Always alone.

Old Foot had told him the legend, one evening when the two of them had made camp up on the Three Brothers, the three mountains that were west of where the two waters meet . . . Ticonderoga. The grandfather had made fire, and before sleep came to share it with them, Old Foot had sung the ancient song of the Rabbit God. A rabbit never cried or screamed, only at death . . . one single cry. The legend said that instead the rabbit wept for others. Then the boy and the old man danced the Dance of the Rabbit God, with steps that were soft and quick.

Standing astride the still head of his deer, ankle-deep in a cloud of red water, Fawn raised his face to the sky. He wished that Old Foot were still alive and could look down and see his kill, He hoped that the old Mohawk warrior would sing in peace up in his lodge beyond the clouds.

Two

The trout would be his evening meal. The deer was too fresh-killed, too warm with life to be eaten on this day.

Bending his back as he had bent his bow, Fawn had to drag the forkhorn up from the shallows of the lake onto the bank among the white birches. Cutting three stout poles, each almost twice his height, he bound the three tips together with strips of bark, and at their joining he lashed them to the antlers of the deer. The wet animal lay at the center of a Y, and as he pushed at the single pole, the tripod went erect. It hung a deer that was heavy with water, antlers up, which he could not have lifted alone. Tonight it would hang. Come dawn, he would lighten the deer by removing the internals, so that he could shoulder it home. My father will be proud, he thought, to see his young son return with a deer on his shoulder. And there will be more deer to bear home, so that we both will feast. Never again will my father see me eat while his own belly howls with hunger. No more will his hands be raw and bleeding from digging down through the winter snow to tear roots from the frozen earth, so that we would not starve.

Fawn made a fire.

Finding a hollow cedar tree, he reached inside for the reddish-brown bark that was old and dry. Rolling it between his hands, Fawn turned it to a powdery pile of tinder on a flat rock. From the pouch at his waist he took flint and steel, striking a red-hot spark into the pile of light bark. Snatching up the pile quickly in his hands, he blew with a gentle but continued breath until the tinder burst to a flame. Adding dry leaves (also taken from inside the cedar) and small twigs, he made fire enough to slowly roast the trout.

A cooking fire, Old Foot always told him, is a small fire, as its aim is to cook and not to burn. Fawn's first fire-meal that he had himself cooked had been a gray squirrel. The fire had been too hot, making the meat charred and black on the outside and raw inside. Old Foot had laughed.

As he cooked the trout, turning over and over the green stick that held it, Fawn thought of how his grandfather had made fire with a bow and spindle, using an old bird's nest for tinder. Old Foot had not used flint and steel, and thought them to be just two more things to carry. Two things he did not need. Things that reminded the old man of the French at the fort. According to the legend, since the coming of Champlain, a hundred and fifty years ago, the Mohawk will hate the French. Old Foot was a Mohawk who would spit on the ground whenever he talked of the French, or the Huron.

With one exception.

It was strange, Fawn thought, the hostile friendship that had existed between Old Foot and his father, a Mohawk and a Frenchman . . . the old warrior and the French scholar, Henri Charbon, who had once been a Jesuit priest. Both have told me the story. Two stories, as different as the fox and the wolf. And now the melting of many winters stirs the two stories into one, and the tale ends with me, Fawn Charbon.

Old Foot had never called Fawn's father Henri. It was always "Black Robe," the man who had come south from Quebec, down Lake Champlain to the land of the Mohawk. He came in peace, without a musket yet not without courage. Not a man of battle but a man of books. Old Foot was too much warrior to draw his bow on such a man. At least not at once. Henri had come from the north, the forest place called Canada; and Old Foot had wished to learn of this land which, according to Mohawk legend, was the home of the great white bear.

Henri had not come alone, but with one Huron guide, the two of them in a Huron canoe. Soon after they came to the upper lake, they were captured by Old Foot and his hunting party, and the Huron did not live long. Joy filled Old Foot's heart as he had watched and heard the Huron die and die slowly. He had no use for a Huron. But Henri spoke in the tongue of the British, which Old Foot could also speak, having heard the English words from the soldiers who wore the red coats long before Fort William Henry was built, the stone home of British warriors. And so Old Foot found reason to spare the Black Robe, for the moment, as curiosity bested hatred.

Old Foot asked Henri Charbon about Canada. How tall was the great white bear? How many days to Canada by canoe? How many Huron, the sons of dogs? Were there Frenchmen with guns and war houses of stone? Henri answered. But more, he then asked questions about the Mohawk, the mighty hunters whose arrows slay the deer. Knowing he would die, Henri was resolute to die well and without fear.

Fawn knew that his father and grandfather slowly became the "enemies that talk," for each knew things that were strange to the other. His father had been taken to a Mohawk village. There he was bound to a stout pine, and beaten. Near death, he had begged for water. And water had been refused him by all Mohawk save one. Her name was Blue Voice, the daughter and only child of Old Foot. Even after Old Foot had beaten her for her kindness, she fed the Black Robe food. Her next punishment for her defiance of her father was being ordered by Old Foot to become the Black Robe's woman. For both Blue Voice and Henri, it was mate or die. No Mohawk would mate with her, as Blue Voice did not walk as others walked, because of a twisted foot. She was worthy only to be the woman of a French Jesuit, a Black Robe. Old Foot had spoken, commanding the union. With whips and stones the two were driven from the Mohawk village, to a faraway cave. They had only each other, for a fall and winter and spring.

And then Blue Voice gave Old Foot a grandchild. Black Robe would live. And as the green of summers turned into the white of many winters, Henri no longer wore his soutane, the black dress. He now wore the skin of the deer and the warm fur of the beaver, and was a Black Robe no more. Old Foot nodded his blessing. The worm had become a butterfly. But now, Fawn thought, turning the trout over the fire, there is no Blue Voice to softly sing. She died of the cold when Fawn was only ten summers. Old Foot had been dead almost a moon. Now there is only father and son, Henri Charbon and Fawn. And the hair of my father grows white as the winter fur of the red weasel, and his soul as lonely as the night wind. Since the death of my mother he has laughed little, and often wept. His talks with Old Foot became arguments between two old men. He would not hunt with us, or fish, and so Old Foot and I became the two who talked.

This deer, Fawn thought, will brighten my father's heart. And together we will prepare it, eat all we can and smoke what is left. It may fill his spirit as well as his belly. I will talk French with him and listen to the stories of his beloved builder, Jesus, told to my father by his friend and teacher, Brother Anthony. And I shall even pretend to understand for I know how it will please him.

As he ate the sweet white flesh of the trout, Fawn Charbon reached inside his pouch to see if the tiny cross his father had given him was still there. It was. It meant little to him, yet he would carry it always to honor his father, to respect him; as his mother, Blue Voice, had respected Old Foot.

Fawn stopped eating to spit out a bone. The trout was good and hot. But his next evening meal would be venison from the forkhorn, a meal he would share with his father. And as we eat, our talk will sauce the meat. Nearby the deer hung motionless, and Fawn looked at it with joy. He was happy that he made the kill with a bow and not a musket. It would have been too easy with a gun, he thought. He had heard that a boy of only fourteen, a French boy who lived at Fort Carillon, had killed a young doe. White boys needed muskets, he thought; but he did not. He was half white, but that was enough. His skin was as Mohawk as Blue Voice and Old Foot.

I am Mohawk, said his heart.

Growing up, he talked much to Old Foot, in Mohawk; and it was as soft as his mother's singing. They spoke as the wind to leaves, as the brook to pebbles. Mohawk words were happy words, so light and clean they flew from the mouth like tiny wrens. English and French had to be written into the earth by a pointed stick.

For a while his father had made him attend school at Fort Carillon, where he had been the only boy with no hair. His father had asked him to let his hair grow, but Fawn would not do this. A Mohawk hunter shaved his head with a knife until it was bald as stone. Except for the topknot. His skin was red like the leaves before winter. The French boys at the fort were white. It was a sick white. Old Foot looked better dead than white men while they still lived.

Fawn had folded a small pot from the bark of a white birch, using a thorn as a pin to hold it fast. The water in the pot was now boiling. The bark would not burn as long as it was filled with lakewater. Opening his waist pouch, Fawn pulled out a tiny sack of tea and sugar. Adding both at once to the bubbling water, he took the bark pot from the orange coals. He had traded a mink pelt for the tea, and the woman with whom he had made the exchange also gave him a pinch of sugar.

Tea! Hot tea with sugar made a good drink, even though it was a white man's drink. French soldiers at the fort drank tea, and some even added a few drops of cow's milk to cool it. Fawn did not. Milk clouded the tea, in color and in taste. Trout and hot tea with sugar made a fine meal on a cool evening. He was cold. He owned a shirt of deerskin that he had made himself, but he had left it behind this morning. Fawn wore only a loincloth, leggings, and mocs on his feet. All were wet.

Using his knife, he cut two large sheets of green moss. One to lie upon and one to lie under. The moss was still damp from the rain, but the heat of his body and the fire would soon dry it. Growing up through the moss were tiny plants of wintergreen. The leaves were small shiny ovals of flavor. Happy leaves. Fawn chewed on one as he added wet wood to his fire and prepared his spirit for sleep, asking the dark sky to be a safe blanket for his father.

During the night, the fire burned out. But even alone in the dark, Fawn told himself that he felt no fear. He would like to see one of the French boys from Fort Carillon dare to sleep alone, without a blanket or a gun. He smiled, remembering that he was half French. Closing his eyes, he rolled his other hip against the hard ground.

Many summers ago he had been sleeping out on a hunt with Old Foot, and he had complained to the old man that his earth bed was hard. Old Foot said that, yes, the ground was hard and so Fawn must make his spine even harder.

Holding his knees up close to his chest, he slept as he had seen his grandfather sleep . . . Old Foot, the Mohawk.

Three

Before the sun was fully up and even before he opened his eyes, he heard the ghosts. And their singing seemed to Fawn to come from a long way off, and still faintly be everywhere.

As his blue eyes opened, looking up to where the yellow sky of morning hit only the tops of the trees, the whispering sound seemed no louder, no closer. Rolling from his bed of moss, he looked out across the lake. Nothing. The water was still, the leaves were still; but the air was full. The tiny strange sound persisted, making Fawn cover his ears. He had heard from Old Foot the legend of the locusts, when the swarm of tiny-winged grasshoppers had come and gone, and with them all of the corn, and the trees were left bare. Yet no insect could cause a sound such as this. Fawn swallowed the nothing in his throat, but the singing did not stop. It went on and on; as if it could not end for it had never begun.

Fawn hurried, ripping the belly of the deer.

Even gutted, the buck was heavy. Fawn's canoe sat low in the water. But it was a strong canoe of birch bark that he and Old Foot had made together, and he knew it would hold. It was unfortunate that the wind blew south. It would not push his canoe north toward Ticonderoga, where the two waters meet. It was there that the small upper Lake (on which Fawn now paddled) became LaChute, as his father called it, foaming down over the rocks in falls and rapids until the waters of LaChute were no longer white, pouring without hurry into the big lake at the fort. The French called the big lake Champlain. Its waters were warmer. Fawn preferred the clear cold spring-fed water of the upper lake. No Frenchman swam here, and the lake was fit to drink.

At the other end of the lake, over a day's canoe to the south, was Fort William Henry, built and held by the English. Old Foot called them the Yengeese, the Yankees. Old Foot could not say "English." Nor did he much care for the British at Fort William Henry. Yet he had been a scout for them. It had been Old Foot who had told the British about the French and their Fort Carillon to the north, at the Ticonderoga end of his lake the English called Lake George, naming it after their White Father, who was King George of England. Around the neck of Old Foot they had hung a small medal of bronze that bore the picture of George the White Father. Old Foot wore the medal until he died; but not to please the British. He wore it to taunt his daughter's man, Henri Charbon, as Fawn had sometimes worn the tiny French cross to tease his Mohawk grandfather.

Fawn Charbon would not be French. Never, he thought.

Perhaps he would learn which French soldier from the fort had fired his musket and wounded Old Foot so that it took the old man three nights to die. Thinking of the French soldiers and their fat wives at the fort, Fawn spat into the lake. But the taste of poison in his mouth was still there.

Tonight, however, he would taste the deer. He and his father would eat their fill, inviting no one from the fort to share it. No one, Fawn thought; as no one ever invited his father to dine at a family table. We are toads to talk to them, even to trade with them. Why does it mean so much to my father that they are French? He means so little to them. We were here first, long before the engineers came to build the fort. Let *them* seek the approval of Henri Charbon. Let them crawl to him, hungry for his company. Let them beg at *his* feet.

Fawn, you dream.

He knew the forkhorn would weight his canoe, and it would be cooler to paddle north before the sun was high. This was the reason Fawn gave himself for his rush. And then the wind changed, the singing of the spirits came louder, making his skin wet. The spot where he slew the deer was a tiny inlet, a hidden retreat from the body of Lake George. Sinking his paddle, his canoe shot out from under the overhang of white birch that kept him and his craft unseen.

Then he saw the gunboats to the south, like tiny waterbugs on their backs with their legs to the side. Not spirits, not a choir of locusts, but men in red coats.

Yengeese! Boats and boats of them, low in the water with the weight of many soldiers. And the wail? Fawn remembered the stories of Old Foot, and his father had told him of the British and their wails of war. What were they called? Now he remembered. Bagpipes. Backing quickly, Fawn stilled his canoe behind the lace of birch leaves and counted the gunboats full of Redcoats. With them were ten canoes of Mohawk scouts. Behind them were even more gunboats carrying men in cloth and deerskin. Every white man, whether he wore a red coat or not, held a musket, except for those who worked the oars. Had they seen him? He fit an arrow to his bow.

Old Foot had been to Fort William Henry many times and had seen the British in their red coats. One of the English men had allowed Old Foot to try on his red tunic. He had told Fawn how he had pretended to be honored, so as not to offend the Englishman. It would be unwise, Old Foot had told Fawn, to make enemies of the British. Fawn's father had said the same. The French were traders and the Dutch to the south were farmers. The Huron were "eaters of bark." But the British, Old Foot and Henri Charbon agreed

. . . the British are like the Mohawk. The British are warriors.

Fawn had once asked Old Foot how a Scottish bagpipe sounded, as the old man had heard them at Fort William Henry. Holding his nose, Old Foot had sung out a weird song that seemed, to Fawn's ear, to be a song of a strange world. He had laughed at Old Foot trying to be a bagpipe. Yet as his grandfather hummed, bumps rose on his flesh.

Now he heard the pipes clearly, a swarm of sound from every gunboat that bore the British soldiers. The air over Lake George was alive with the war cry of pipes. Fawn's father had once talked with an old French soldier who had heard the bagpipes play on an evening before battle between the English and the French. The old soldier had called them "the sting of Scottish bees." As a youth he had heard them, and the pipes would haunt his sleep forever.

Frozen low in his canoe, motionless, Fawn listened to the drones and chanters of a thousand pipes, wailing a tune without beginning or end. The bumps came again. He imagined that cold moss grew on the spine of many an enemy soldier who had heard the wail creeping closer and closer through the mist, like a death before the battle, played by unseen pipers.

The British were here, as Old Foot said they would come. As his father had also said they would come and come and come, until the waters of the upper lake and the lower lake turned red with French and English blood. And the Mohawk, allies of the British, would be caught between. Like the Huron, who were scouts of the French. The Huron, too, would die.

Fawn guessed that the British Redcoats and their English-speaking colonials were headed north to LaChute, to portage there and attack the French at Fort Carillon. The French would know, too; for the Huron were the eyes and ears of the French. Already, Fawn thought, Huron eyes had looked down from the great rock shoulders of the upper lake and had seen the al-

most endless rows of whaleboats rowing north. Huron
fingers had pointed down from the pines. What, he
wondered, would Huron ears hear when they heard
British bagpipes? Were the pipes the singing of
women over braves fallen in battle? Blue Voice had
said that the ghosts of warriors walked the waters of
the lower lake, the ghosts of dead and defeated Hurons on their way north to the place called Canada.
On windy nights, she heard the songs of dead Huron.
It could have sounded no worse, thought Fawn, than
the pipes and the drums of the red-coated British, the
Yengeese.

Mohawk would not attack so, with music. Nor
would Huron. Nor would the French, who learned to
fight concealed as the Huron fought. Only the British
would sing on the way to battle, and only the British
would tell of their coming to the enemy with drum
and pipe. The marching sting of Scottish bees.

Even though his back was soon covered by a swarm
of white aphids that fell from the leaves, all day long
Fawn Charbon stayed still, keeping his canoe from
making even a ripple in his blind of birch. And all day
long the gunboats passed his hiding, boat after boat.
All of England, Fawn thought. All of England has
come north to Ticonderoga to kill the French. All the
Yankees have come to slay the great General Montcalm.

He must get home!

The British and the Mohawk might find my father,
he thought, and my father is French. If only Old Foot
were still alive and there with him. Old Foot would
know what to do. There were times to fight and times
to run, his grandfather had said to him. Even the
skunk gives ground to the great owl. But his father
might not have such wisdom, for how could wisdom
be found in books? Or in rum? The skunk neither
read nor drank strong drink, and yet he was wise. At
this moment, Fawn Charbon would have been

pleased had his father had no more than the sense of the skunk.

The sun was low when the last group of British gunboats rowed by the inlet where Fawn Charbon and his canoe and deer were hidden. Fawn's body ached from holding his position for so long a time. Yet had he moved more than to blink his blue eyes, a hundred muskets could have sent a hundred balls of lead into the leafy blind. One skunk, thought Fawn . . . one skunk dares not challenge the talons of so many great owls.

The last gunboat held no Redcoats, just colonials and two Mohawk. It was a small boat that took only four oarsmen. One of the four rowed with his shirt off, and Fawn could see how young he was. A mere forkhorn. A boy of his own age, and not more than seventeen summers. The boy's chest was white; and hairless like his own, not furry like the broad chests of some of the Yankee men.

But suddenly the boat turned, its bow pointing toward where Fawn and his canoe were heavy in the water behind the blind of birch. Closer, closer . . . until Fawn pulled back his bow. Then he saw the reason. One of the men had stopped pulling his oar as the boat had broken through a large and active swarm of gnats, the black flies that bite as bees. The man in the stern even dropped his tiller to ward off the attacking insects, causing the boat to drift without direction.

Fawn could have sent an arrow through the white boy's back that was now black with bugs. But even though some of the men stopped rowing to fight off the flies, the boy had never stilled his oar. Bitten and bitten, he continued to row. The tillerman corrected his heading and the boat passed out of sight.

The boy has courage, Fawn thought. Old Foot would nod.

Four

It was dark. Fawn Charbon had taken his canoe as far north on Lake George as he dared to go.

Ahead of him, at the place where the portage path twisted down the hill to the lower lake, Fawn saw the many orange specks that were the fires of the British camp. The fires were in number like the stars. He moved his paddle in a circle, never lifting it from the water. The slap of a paddle could be heard, so Fawn glided quietly.

Reaching the small marsh where he often hid his canoe, he carried the forkhorn to shore, pushing the empty canoe deep among the reeds. Buried inside the stand of cattails, the canoe would not be seen unless by accident. Fawn and Old Foot had cut the canoe, and on its hull the old man had burned the bark with the sign of a black turtle. Old Foot was a Mohawk of the Turtle Clan. If the Mohawk who were with the British found the canoe, perhaps they would spare it. But the Huron and the French would destroy it.

While taking the deer to shore, Fawn's foot slipped once on a mossy stone. His moc slapped the water! Dropping to the shallows at the lake's edge, he lay cold among the reeds and did not move until he saw the moon pass behind the trunk of a beech tree.

Moving softly through the trees with the stiff deer thrown across his shoulder, he saw campfires on all sides of him. None were close. Several times he heard the rattle of powder tins and musketry. The British would not hear him, so busy were they with their

preparations for meeting the French. But the Mohawk? Their eyes would be everywhere, and their
ears. And if their senses could not stab through the
darkness, Mohawk arrows could. Fawn had seen Old
Foot snap his bowstring, aiming only at sound in the
night, and his arrow had found the empty belly of a
panther.

"A lucky shot," his grandfather had said in Mohawk. Fawn knew better. The old man did not believe
in luck. Old Foot believed in Old Foot and his bow.

Working step by step through the night, Fawn took
a well-hidden portage path that led down to the
lower lake to avoid the falls, LaChute. Here it could
be risky, he thought, perhaps foolish to run down the
path. No doubt the British had sent their Mohawk
scouts down the trail. And not only the Mohawk
would be about. The Huron were braver, now that
the French had built the fort at the mouth of La-
Chute. The Huron were his enemies, as they had been
the enemies of Old Foot. The old man had warned
him that it was best to stay away from the Mohawk as
well as the Huron. Fawn wanted to know why he
should fear the Mohawk. Old Foot had then bared his
knife and cut the boy's arm. With his mouth over the
tiny wound, Old Foot sucked a mouthful of blood and
then spat it on the ground. "French blood," said Old
Foot. "That is why."

The forkhorn buck was heavy.

Out of breath from the young deer on his shoulder,
Fawn Charbon stopped to rest in the darkness. Perhaps he should not have been so proud, he thought,
and left the deer behind to be eaten by the wolves.
No, he must bring the deer home to show his father.
This was not just any meat. It was his first deer. My
father, he thought, will be pleased. Perhaps once
again his heart will be happy.

Standing on the rock ledge that overlooked the
lower falls of LaChute, he let the buck slide from his

shoulder. His legs ached. The forkhorn was not so
heavy when he had first started down from the upper
lake, down the portage path. But it seemed to gain in
weight, and his breath blew harder.

He lay down on the flat rocks that overlooked La-
Chute, glad it was dark and he could come home unseen. Looking at the white water was good. It was a
place to stop and catch his breath. LaChute, his father
had named it. Old Foot called it Ticonderoga. But
when the old man spoke in English, the tongue of the
Yengeese, Old Foot called it Two Waters. The place
between the two blue lakes, Fawn thought, where the
water is white. LaChute is angry.

Lake George, he thought as he watched the falls
foam, is angry to meet Lake Champlain. The cold angry British water on its way to do battle below with
the calm French water of the lower lake, Champlain.
Fawn was born here, between the Two Waters. As he
grew up, there had only been the four: Old Foot, Blue
Voice, Henri and himself. How quiet it had been. The
French soldiers and engineers had not yet come to
build Fort Carillon.

He could not rest here at the falls for long. There
was no time. The British had come, to take General
Montcalm and his fortress. Fawn was tired. But tonight was not the time to think of sleep. Shouldering
the buck once more, Fawn Charbon took a last look at
the boiling water of LaChute, a field of white bub-
bles that grew in the darkness. Crossing over the
creek on a family of flat rocks, he started down the
hill that gently sloped away from the falls, heading
east into the valley of Champlain. He trotted. The
roar of LaChute grew soft, then quiet. Fawn heard
another sound. The noise of axes on trees and many
soldiers shouting in French came from the direction of
the fort.

Fawn must see.

Dropping his deer quickly, he ran along the trail

toward the noise. Coming closer, Fawn saw the torches burning. He saw a large tree quiver and then fall. Men were chaining several yoke of oxen to the trees, dragging them into some odd kind of pile. The butts all pointed toward the fort, but the top branches pointed away.

Women and girls were working with small hatchets, some with kitchen knives; and as they worked, the small branches of the felled trees became sharpened spears. Tree upon tree went down. Ox after ox hauled the timber into the strange line with all its white points, freshly hewn, pointing up the gentle hill at the place from where the British would come.

Montcalm was preparing.

Fawn had seen General Montcalm a number of times, but had spoken to him only once. It was the day after Old Foot died, and Fawn was sitting on a rock, throwing small pebbles into the quiet muddy water of the lower lake. A voice behind him spoke in French, and he had turned around to see the thin, handsome general in his white uniform. A blue cloak was over his shoulders.

"How far," he asked Fawn in French, "can you throw one of your stones?"

"Not very far."

"Show me."

It was a command from Montcalm, delivered in a quiet voice. And so Fawn threw a stone for the general.

"Good," said the soldier. "But let me show you how we would throw stones when I was a little boy in France. We used to look around for a flat one. Ah! Just like this. And then, with an underhand whip of the arm . . . like so! See? It skips. Once, twice, again and again until the skips are no bigger than the tiny steps of a little dance. You try."

Fawn Charbon had then, he remembered, skipped a stone for the great Montcalm. And then the general had thrown another.

"How do you hold it?" Fawn asked, remembering a saying of his father that a man who hates too much often learns too little.

"Like so," said General Montcalm, "with the thumb and one finger only. The stone is round, you see. And so, like the wheel of a wagon, it rolls off the finger, and the whip of your arm gives the stone its speed."

The general threw a third stone.

"What is your name? I believe I know who you are?"

"I am Fawn."

"Fawn, eh? That is all?"

"Fawn Charbon."

"Ah! The son of Henri, the scholarly woodsman. Your father taught you to speak excellent French. My boy, you dress as a red savage, but you are a Frenchman."

"I am Mohawk, sir."

"Mohawk? Ah, no! For were this true, here in the valley of the French and the Huron, you would be a very dead Mohawk. Or, to say as much, a very captured one. Your mother is a Mohawk woman?"

"I am the son of Blue Voice, and the grandson of Old Foot. But now my grandfather is dead, because of one of your soldiers."

"I am sorry. You and your grandfather were close friends, eh?"

"Yes. He was a Mohawk, and I am a Mohawk."

"True. *And* a Frenchman."

General Montcalm walked on; slowly, as if he had much thinking to do. Was he wondering when this night would come, when the British would come?

Fawn had seen enough of the felling of trees. The French soldiers, it seemed, would prepare all night for the British. He returned, and threw the deer over his back. Walking through the stand of pines, he neared the well-hidden clearing that encircled the small bark house where he had lived ever since remembering. Cupping his hand to his mouth, he made the lonely cry of a loon. It was his signal. His father would answer with bold whistle of a red-crested bird, which he called a cardinal, someone who wore a robe of red.

Fawn waited. But he heard no answer.

Five

The rum was gone.

Henri Charbon sat on the straw floor of his bark house. Evening had passed and the night had come; so he sat in the dark, slowly scratching his thick beard, with only his thoughts for company.

Was there, he wondered, ever a place called France? Or were his boyhood and early priesthood just a dream, as if they had never happened. And to think that the people at the fort, almost within hollering, actually called this black wilderness by the name of New France. Well, at least with Fort Carillon so near, he and Fawn were not totally alone. Socially alone, but not as geographically isolated as before. I am free, he thought, to visit the fort, but never am I a part of it nor am I one of them. They know. I can feel it when they look at me. I can almost hear their whispers of disapproval:

"There goes the Jesuit who lived with a Mohawk woman, not even a Huron. Have you seen that son of his who is half white and half red? There he goes, back into the shadows where he belongs, for only there can Henri Charbon hide his face and drink away his shame."

Henri reached for the rum bottle. Empty, as empty as I. May the Devil take my curse, my thirst. And there is no fire by which to read my breviary.

Seventeen years, Henri thought. And still I carry it with me. When I sleep, my little breviary is in my hand, worn though it is. How well I remember when I

first received it as a young priest, a gift from Brother
Anthony. On the book's black cover, in gold leaf, were
stamped four letters: A.M.D.G. *Ad maiorem dei glo-
riam.* "To the greater glory of God," the motto of the
Jesuits.

Tightly in his hands, Henri Charbon held the little
black book, as he often did when he was by himself.
If only Fawn were here. Or my woman, my Blue
Voice.

One day, Henri thought, one day Fawn will leave as
a young swallow who flies from the nest and will
never return and I shall die alone. And when he goes I
pray him safe journey and Godspeed. Last night,
Fawn did not return from hunting. And now, night is
again here and I have no son. Does he know? Could
he possibly know that he is all I have and my only
reason for living?

Someday, perhaps, Fawn will be a father and he
will be feeling what I now feel. How we reach out for
our offspring, with such desperation, and yet they do
not know what we feel for them or even if we feel at
all. Until he himself has sired a son who goes hunting
and does not return for two sunsets. *Then* he will long
for his child, and know too late how I, his father, now
long for him. Just to see the sunshine of his face or
hear the music of his voice.

Perhaps Fawn is alone and hurt. No! I must not
think such a thought. Fawn is the grandson of Old
Foot, and in the breast of this boy the spirit of his
grandfather still survives. Were that the boy were my
son, rather than that old man's grandchild. Nay to
that. A selfish thought. What better teacher could
Fawn have had in this wild and Godless classroom,
and who but Old Foot could have better instructed
the lad in how to live in a place where so many others
die?

Even as a tot Fawn sang the songs of the Mohawk,
and danced the Mohawk dances. Day by day, the old
devil stole my child from me. Hunt by hunt, kill by

kill, legend upon legend, he painted the boy with Mohawk paint until there is no white on his body and no French in his soul. And so, as I discarded my priestly robe to live as an animal, my child is more animal than any beast. There is nothing of the classic Frenchman in him, and little of his mother. And nothing, thank God, nothing of him that is Henri Charbon.

And yet, behind those stone blue eyes of his there is intelligence. His awareness, his facility with language. Fawn could speak with the King of France with the same ease that he grunted with Old Foot. To think how I struggled with my Latin verbs. Little enough good ever came of it. One swallow, one hot wet swallow of French rum, Henri thought, is worth every Latin verb copied by all the monks of Christendom.

Here I sit alone. As we have always been alone, afraid to talk in French for fear the Mohawk will hear; and in English for fear of the Huron. I am afraid; as I have yet not to be afraid in this unholy wilderness, alone with my ability to recite Cicero. A useless talent. Without Fawn's bow we would starve, or beg like crippled curs at the kitchen door of a soldier's mess. What could I provide, except to catch frogs and dig up roots? All the dreams I had to take my son to France, and to show him art and see his face when he first hears a cello in a noble court. Dreams, and no more. How could I return? The bridge is burned and there is no return except to my own disgrace. The music that is mine is only the evening wind and the strange voices that whisper into the deafening ears of old men who wait to die.

Time, where does it go as it races by in daylight and in darkness? Day, dark, day, dark. Time does little but age us. How old is Fawn? Henri Charbon, do you forget the age of your child? And to think it was I who taught him the seven days, the twelve months, the year 1758. We are in July, but here in New France there is no July, and thus the great clock ticks on, beating away like the heart of God.

Looking up suddenly, Henri Charbon was aware that a man stood in the doorway and the shape moved toward him. The axe, where was it? Quickly he held up his hands to ward off the blow he knew would come. But instead he heard a soft voice, almost a blue voice.

"Father?"

Fawn whispered in French; and as he did so, Henri Charbon looked up. Long ago his eyes had failed to see clearly, but he knew the voice and the smell of his son.

"Fawn! Fawn, you are safe."

"Of course I am safe. But please, Father, we must not raise our voices. The woods crawl with Mohawk."

"Fawn, you've killed a deer! Your first." Henri rose to his feet.

"Yes, Father, a forkhorn. Not large but tender and our cooking pot will bubble with meat."

"I am proud of you, Fawn. A pity that your grand-father is not alive to see; and your mother, too. And *what* a deer!"

As he spoke, Henri Charbon saw the lean shoulders of his son straighten with pride. Fawn's body was sil-ver in the moonlight. Could it be that the boy had grown in two days?

"You sweat," he said to Fawn.

"The deer is heavy. Father, I think it best that we go north and away from the fort."

"But we are safe here. This is our home. The Mo-hawk have come before, and to them we speak En-glish. And to the Huron, French. They have all come before."

"Yes, Father, they have come before. And once we had the bow of Old Foot to turn them away. And the rank of Old Foot which they respected. But now, Fa-ther, you have only Fawn. And Fawn will take his fa-ther and his deer and go. This time the Mohawk are many and their faces are colored with the white paint of war."

Henri looked about, knowing that he wished to take his books. His foot kicked the empty rum bottle. Fawn bent down, picked up the bottle, and without a word he threw it into the trees. Fawn did not mention this bottle, nor all the others.

"Must we go tonight?" Henri asked.

"Yes, for the British have come with an army. And you are French."

"The *British* have come? Are you sure?"

"Yes, they come like ants surprised in a rotted tree. Tomorrow the flag of France may burn, and we will see British colors flying from the same pole."

"You think the British will defeat *Montcalm?*"

"All day long I watch the British go north on Lake George. Counting them, I reached a thousand for fifteen times. Until dark I heard the thunder of their drums and cry of their pipes, and to my ear it was more madness than music. The British and their Yengeese colonials are many and the French are few. Besides, the British have the Mohawk. General Montcalm has only the Huron."

"We were here first. And we did not run from the Mohawk, the French or the Huron. Why should we run now from the British? If I am to die, Fawn, let me die under a French flag as a soldier, instead of in the forest as a fugitive. If the British and the Mohawk come in such numbers, then General Montcalm can use me at Fort Carillon."

"You are not a soldier, Father."

"No, I am no soldier. And I am no priest. Blue Voice is dead and I am not a husband. To you, not even a father. But tomorrow, let me live one more day as a true Frenchman."

"Your life is yours, to keep or give. But when the British and the Mohawk come as countless spiders, you will be in the web as a helpless fly."

Henri felt, for a passing moment, that Fawn was about to reach out and place a restraining hand on his shoulder. He waited, but the touch did not come.

Fawn's face showed nothing. Once again inside his breast, Henri Charbon felt himself cursing the old Mohawk warrior who had hardened his own grandson into oak.

"Then," said Henri, "I will be the fly that fights. I go willingly to the web and take my stand. I can fire a musket. If the British are in number as you say, perhaps one or two less Redcoats will live to tear down French colors."

"Brave talk. Will you talk with such courage when the British soldiers throw you like a toy to the Mohawk? Did you listen to Old Foot so little that you know not whom the French came to slaughter? Justice to the ear of Old Foot was a Frenchman's scream."

His voice is cold Henri thought. He speaks to me with conviction and with reason and his words are even, without temper. Can he neither hate nor love?

"My life is mine, what little is left of it. I am going to the fort, whether you come or not. Whether I go as a fighter or a fool is yet to unfold," said Henri.

"We are fools to stand here and do neither. Go to the fort if you want."

"And will *you* come?"

"Only to see you to the wall. No farther. I will leave you there. We will take my deer to say that we bring meat. If the British come and take you captive, better you are a Frenchman in a British dungeon than in a Mohawk camp. You speak the tongue of the Yengeese with ease. But your voice runs with Mohawk like the gait of a three-legged cow."

"Fawn? Please stay the night at the fort."

"You know I do not sleep near the stink of unwashed Huron. Or near the beds of Frenchmen who kill old men."

"As you wish."

"Here is my knife, Father. Will you cut a tote pole?"

"A pole. For what reason?"

"So that you and I may carry the deer between us.

Let the French see it is Henri Charbon who brings meat. I will bind the legs."

Upside down by its legs on the pole, the deer hung stiff with death. Fawn walked first, with the front end of the staff on his shoulder. Henri followed a staff-length behind. He saw little in the dark, so he was content to follow in the steps of the boy until they were close to the fort.

"I must tell General Montcalm that the British have come," said Henri.

"Listen. The sound of many axes will tell you that your great general already knows, as the Huron have seen this day what I have seen. Even though my eyes have seen it, my mind says it was a dream. And my ears deny the evil wail of their singing."

"The pipes! You heard the Scottish pipes?"

"I heard. Nothing human and nothing animal could make such a sound. It is neither singing nor crying, but rather a disease in the wind that drives a fever into the ear."

"Where will you go?"

"To the upper lake. And when the sun comes, I will watch all of you destroy each other like a pack of wolves bitten by the summer sickness. But first I must see the Yengeese in their camp. And from the darkness where I will not be seen, I will study the Mohawk. This is my chance to learn."

"You wish to learn about the Mohawk and the *English?*"

Fawn turned to look at his father. "Yes, to learn."

Setting down his pole, Fawn threw the deer onto the back of his father. "You are safe. Go alone. Tell them you bring meat to feed French soldiers. It will take the British a day to reach this place, but only part of a day to destroy it. Here you fight and here you die."

"Are you to join the Mohawk? Join *us* instead."

"Fawn joins no one. This is not France, and I am not a Frenchman."

Deep in his belly, Henry Charbon felt a stab of hatred for his son. Pup without reason. Now is our chance, our chance to be Frenchmen again; this time forever! But no, this child casts it all away.

"Be an animal, then . . . like your grandfather! Go be some grunting Mohawk beast in a cave without a flag and *never* be a Frenchman."

"You forget, Father."

"Forget? Forget what?"

"It was not Fawn who chose a Mohawk mother. It was you who chose a Mohawk mate."

"Yes, I chose your mother and I do not regret the choice I made. Rome was far off, and your mother was by my side. And so I chose to love your mother more. But at the time, it was more of a decision between taking her or a Mohawk axe. I saw what they did to the one Huron who came with me. They bit into his body, chewed upon his living flesh, and spat the pulp in his face. I watched. It took the Huron two days to die. Two days."

"I know. Old Foot told me the story. Mother was born crippled and needed a husband. Your life was spared. So do not complain, Father. You walked away from a Mohawk camp and you live to look into an evening fire and remember your fear but not forget your fortune."

"I was afraid, yes. As any Englishman would be afraid among the Huron. Had I not made the decision I did, I would not have had Blue Voice, and we would not have had you."

"And you would be dead."

"Yes," said Henri.

"If you die tomorrow, you will not die alone. I have counted the British warriors and I believe many Frenchmen will die. And so I ask you one last time . . . do not be the hare who thrusts his head into the loop. This fort is your snare. Please, Father. We will take my deer and go north, and let the British and French waste each other's lives. Will you come?"

"No. I will fight for France," said Henri. He stood as straight as he could, his head held high.

"You are a stubborn old man. As bad as Old Foot in his last toothless winter. Worse than he, for you choose death to life. So go to your fort. And I hope you fall at the end of a British bayonet rather than fall among Mohawk. If this is your wish, then *die*."

Henri suddenly felt his throat go dry. Was this it? Had all the years added up to not even a good-bye? As Fawn turned without a sound and faded into the forest night, Henri Charbon held the deer with both arms.

But his heart held his son.

Six

Fawn ran through the night, heading west.

Leaving the shadow of Fort Carillon, once again he passed unseen by the breastwork of fallen trees that the French soldiers, under the order of General Montcalm, were erecting. The torches still burned, the trees still fell. And the ring of iron upon wood seemed to be everywhere.

Yokes of oxen were being used to drag the big trees into position. As the oxen passed by one of the torches, Fawn could see the giant animals steam with the strain of work. One ox staggered and fell. A French soldier beat the tired beast with a leather lash until the ox regained his feet. As the torchlight danced on his face, the French corporal seemed as spent as his animals. The great tree seemed wedged against a gray rock that tore from the earth like a large tooth. There were shouts. More men came with a pry log and the tree was freed and moved into its final place in the breastwork.

Near one of the torches, Fawn saw a group of Huron scouts. Their faces seemed clouded in wonder, as if they did not understand the preparations of the French. One Huron pointed at the soldiers who were attacking the trees with steel, shaking his head as if to say the ways of the French were odd, even to their allies, the Huron from the north.

Fawn moved quietly among the shadows. Step by step, the sound of the men felling trees grew fainter and fainter, until all he now heard was the distant voice of LaChute, the waterfall.

At the lodge of his father he stopped only long enough to put on his shirt of deerskin. And to hide the axe.

About to leave the hut, he saw the things that belonged to his father. He would save them. But why? Tomorrow his father would be dead and need them no longer. Yet in the event that his father were to live, to escape, he would return for his treasures. And if I cannot save my father's life, Fawn thought, then let it be said I saved the things that he lived for . . . and will perhaps even die for. Finding an old sheet of deerskin, he did what had to be done. Then he left.

Soon, thought Fawn, the British charge down from the upper lake to meet Montcalm. This I must see, the defeat of all Frenchmen. Including my father? No. But if he is to die, let him choose the ground. He is old, and winter cannot be spring.

Upstream from the lower falls of LaChute, Fawn Charbon moved slowly. His ears strained to hear a sound, any sound. But all he heard was the endless song of bugs and frogs, chirping on and on and on throughout the night. Above him, the British would be sleeping. The Yengeese would be resting for the battle ahead. Or would they drink the rum of the white man, and turn themselves into the three fools? That was what Old Foot said of a man who drank rum. He was a fool in his walk, his mouth, and his head. Old Foot would not drink the white man's rum. To him it tasted like fire. Yet he explained to his grandson why Henri drank rum, as Blue Voice was dead and would sing no more.

Ahead, up the hill, Fawn thought he saw a flicker of light.

Working toward it, he drew closer to where the light had been, but now there was no light. This, Fawn thought, is not to be swallowed. Fires do not make themselves. Then he heard a voice. There were

three voices. Two of them spoke in the scream of
whispers asking the third to be also quiet. But the
third voice spoke in defiance of the stillness.

Fawn could not see the three men, but he knew
they were Huron.

They had been moving through the dense brush,
headed down the mountain toward the fort. But for
some reason they no longer traveled. The three Huron
had stopped to bicker in the night. When one of the
trio did make a fire with a bow and spindle, Fawn
could see. They were not more than five lengths of a
man's body away from where he crouched in a nest of
low juniper. As he waited in the darkness, Fawn
chewed on a smoke-blue berry.

He heard a noise.

It was the slap of a hand. The fire burned brighter,
and Fawn saw their captive. The Hurons had taken
prisoner one of the Yankee colonials, who had probably come north on Lake George along with the huge
army of British. Their prisoner wore boots that were
ankle high, dark stockings and britches, and almost no
shirt. What had once been a white shirt was now in
tatters. A wound on the captive's arm made a wet
flicker of red in the firelight. Fawn decided to wait.
Why should he interfere? His tribe was neither Huron
nor Yankee.

"For the priests," his father had said, "there is the
Society of Jesus. But for a red and white marriage
there is no society. Neither red nor white; not Chris-
tian or heathen."

Old Foot, thought Fawn, had been their only
friend. Perhaps because he respected Henri; but more
likely, because he was the father of Blue Voice. But
now Blue Voice and Old Foot were gone. And no one
at the fort had ever asked his father to come and share
their corn and meat. White doors were closed to a
squaw man. And red doors. No longhouse of the Mohawk would welcome a Frenchman. Not even a Black
Robe. Many a priest, said Old Foot, had been killed

by the Mohawk bow. Fawn had seen the eyes of Old
Foot as he had spoken, and his eyes wore the cold
look. His grandfather would not tell Henri of torturing
the French priests. Old Foot never told all he knew. It
was Fawn's guess that the knife of Old Foot was no
stranger to French blood. And his ears had heard their
helpless crying as they begged for death.

Could there ever be a madness to match the fear of
a white man captured by Mohawk or Huron? Fawn
did not envy the man whose wrists were now being
bound by thongs, securing him to the stout lower
branch of a pine.

Fawn had never seen a man, white or red, tortured.
Once he had been with his father down at the fort;
and in the courtyard, a French soldier was being
flogged. The other soldiers were forced to watch the
man take his punishment. As the lash cut the flesh of
his back, the man's body writhed in torment. The soldier wept. And the faces of the men who watched
wept with him. Later he had told of the episode to his
grandfather. Old Foot said that the ways of the white
man were strange. They did not torture their enemies,
only their own.

Fawn wondered, as he watched the three Huron
sharpen small staffs of wood in the fire, how well the
Yengeese would die. The Huron stripped his body of
all clothing, and he was a cold white figure alone in
the blackness. One of the warriors pulled a burning
torch from the fire. At the tip of the black point there
was a tiny red ember. Approaching the captive Yankee, the Huron held the smoldering wood closer and
closer to the white face.

It was the boy!

Fawn recognized the boy in the boat, the one who
had not stopped pulling on his oar even though the
swarm of black flies covered him. It was that same
resolute face. But this was more than gnats. And yet
the boy did not scream as the fire touched his cheek.

Throwing back his foot, the boy whipped up a stout kick into the crotch of the Huron.

As the warrior doubled over in pain, one of the other two laughed. It was unwise laughter.

The warrior who took the kick suddenly drew his knife. The Huron who had laughed would never again laugh, as his throat was a fountain of blood. The third Huron rushed at the man who had done the killing. His back was to Fawn; but Fawn could see that he too was dead, even before he fell facedown on the fire and did not move. Several breaths later, Fawn smelled the roasting flesh.

The look on the face of the man who held the knife was a look that Fawn had never seen before. The Huron was sick. His face was an illness, infected by his power to ordain death. Two deaths. But now Fawn could not see the crazed face of the Huron, as he had turned his knife upon the boy. He stuck the tip of the bloody blade into the pale naked body. The boy winced, but did not cry out. The Huron was angered. He pushed his knife into the boy's belly, just beneath the point of the breastbone. Fawn knew the boy would be gutted alive with a quick downward slash, just as Fawn had drawn the deer. Fawn thought, could the boy be of use?

There was little time to think. In less than a quick breath an arrow was in his bow and the tightness of the bowstring pressed against the fingertips of his right hand. Is there no difference in killing a Huron than a forkhorn? No, Fawn thought. The moment had come. He had waited for the moment to slay the deer. The drum of his heart said now . . . now . . . now. The arrowhead would thrust deep into the spine of the mad Huron. Yet not in the back.

"Turn around, dog."

His knife still in the belly of the white boy, the Huron jerked about. Perhaps he did not know the French words, but he knew their meaning. This Huron knew that he would not gut his white captive. He fell, twisting on the ground and rolling in the hot ash of the fire, his hands tearing at his own throat, as he died with a Mohawk arrow through his shattered neck.

Fawn's arrow.

Seven

"Who in hell are you?"

The boy was far from dead. Fawn could see, as he stepped from behind the clump of juniper, that the white boy still had blood and spirit. Yengeese do not die easily, Old Foot had once said. There was much life in this boy; even though he was naked, bound to a tree, and with a Huron knife still stuck in his hairless belly.

"I am called Fawn."

"Like a young deer," the boy grunted, fighting his pain.

"Yes."

"You speak English?"

"Some."

"You better pull this here pig sticker out of my guts, or I'm like to die."

"You will not die," said Fawn.

Stepping over the bodies of the three dead Huron warriors, Fawn Charbon placed his hand carefully around the handle of the knife. Slowly he withdrew it from the boy's body. Lucky for the boy, the knife was small. But the short blade was entirely red.

"God! It hurt worse coming out than going in."

"Then I will put it back."

"No thanks. One poke in the gizzard with that there thing is full measure for me, at least for one night. Lordy, am I ever bleeding."

"Good," said Fawn. "It washes clean your wound."

Fawn saw the tiny red streak flow down the boy's

body. Walking to the Huron who had the arrow in his throat, Fawn wiped the blade clean and replaced the knife in the dead man's sheath. The warrior twitched his leg, a movement of death. Do I regret his death? Fawn thought. No, I feel no sorrow. Instead I feel peace that the boy is alive, even though he is a stranger.

"How come you done that? That big old boy won't need a knife where he's going."

"I believe he will," said Fawn. "It is said that a man may hunt and catch fish in the life that follows life. If so, without a blade, it will be hard to clean fish."

"You a friend of them three?"

"Huron dirt. No, I am not a friend of the Huron. No more than you are a friend of General Montcalm."

"Ain't you about to cut me loose? I'm trussed up so cozy to this here hunk of wood, I don't feel a thing in each hand."

"Before I cut you loose, I will learn if you can be of use to me. What is your name?" Fawn came closer to the boy, carrying a torch from the fire.

"Ben."

"You came north with the British, in a boat with men like you and two of the Mohawk. You pulled an oar, along with three others. Are you English?"

"No, I ain't English. I'm American. Boy, if you ain't the queerest son of a ringtail catfish that I ever run across. What in hell are you, some kind of a spook?"

"I am Mohawk."

"But you spoke French to the fellow you cut down on, and you talk English good as me. And you got *blue* eyes."

"Yes. As I am the son of . . . a ringtail catfish."

"It's right by me. You're a true son and heir of a ringtail catfish. Damn, these bugs are eating me up alive, and my hands are choked to purple. You intend to turn me independent or no?"

"Do you wish to return to the camp of the British?"

"Why in holy tarnation would I want to do that?

Not when it's so dang much fun to get naked to a tree with a hundred bugs biting my ass. Where do you want me to go, Mister Fawn? You name it. Just let me go. Or wake up them Hurons, and let me go with *them*."

Fawn was suddenly ashamed. Here he was, letting a wounded boy stand without clothing to be eaten by bugs. With a sudden motion, Fawn drew his own knife. He made two quick slashes near Ben's wrists. He was free.

"Thank you, Mister. Whoever you are, I sure am beholding. Never thought it'd feel so blessed blissful to scratch the bites on my backside."

"It is not wise to scratch the bumps made by bugs. If you raise more blood, more bugs will come. Are you not bloody enough?"

"You mean you don't never scratch yourself? What if they itch?"

"Then I let them itch."

"You ain't got no feelings."

"That is what my father once said, that I do not feel."

"He the ringtail catfish?"

"Yes," Fawn laughed. It was amusing to watch Ben pulling on his britches and trying to scratch at the same time.

"Well," said Ben, "it don't beat my old man. You know what my pa wants *me* to be?"

"No."

"A druggist. Honest now, can you see me in some apothecary store, pushing out purgative pills to a passel of old ladies to shake up their insides and make their bowels belch?"

Such a stream of words. Fawn understood only some of them, and yet Ben was not dull to the ear. Not like the old schoolmaster at the fort. Ben was different. Ben's words made pictures. Words were dull unless they gave color to the eye as well as the ear. Old Foot said that the best words of all were heard in the heart.

"What do you want to be, Ben?"

"A soldier."

"And that is why you come with the Redcoats and their bagpipes, to be a soldier against the French."

"That's why, I reckon. It was either be a druggist back home in Connecticut, or come north and get myself shot by a Frenchie. I figure getting shot was less painful. So I run away from home, joined the colonials, to come north with Abercromby."

"Is he your leader?"

"Yeah, if'n you could call it that. Our second in command is the real ram. Or was. Lord Howe was our brigadier. But he got killed today in a skirmish with the Frenchies and the Indians. I went along with some of our boys, as scouts. Lord Howe weren't more than a spit away from where I was hid, right beside a brook, when he stood up and took a ball in the chest. It must of done his Lordship in as it hit. Broke his back, they said. And busted up his heart and lungs. Then there was more firing. That was when we all sort of scattered off into the woods like a bunch of spooked hens. All of a sudden I was alone in all them trees and I didn't know which way to turn. So I up and hollered a bit, which was a big blunder. On account of which, them three Hurons came out of the woods at me from all sides. So here I am."

"Was this Lord Howe your real general?"

"Sure was. All the regulars, the Redcoats, said he was tops as an officer. Not an old lady like Abercromby. Some even called him Namby Cromby. But not Lord Howe. He was a right fine gentleman. I even heard tell that he carried a snuffbox that was solid silver. His grandfather was George the First, the King of England."

"Will your tribe without red coats follow Abercromby?"

"Maybe," said Ben. "I wouldn't follow that popinjay even if'n he was headed for a bawdy house. And from the looks of the old goat, he wouldn't know what to do if he got there. But with Lord Howe dead, lot of us plain folk just as soon stack our muskets and witness."

"Who will win?"

"British, probably. They always win."

"So do the Mohawk."

"The spot I'm in now," said Ben, "best I agree."

He liked the way Ben spoke English. His father had spoken English in a manner stiff and hard to speak. Ben let it out easy, like a breath after a big meal.

"Best you agree," said Fawn. It felt good to say, and it made his ribs happy.

One of the Huron had been carrying a blue blanket. Lifting it from the ground, Fawn smelled the blanket. It stunk of Huron. He tossed the blanket to Ben.

"Here," he said to Ben, "you will need this to keep the cold from your bones."

"Thanks, Fawn. I guess I owe ya a good turn."

"That is true," said Fawn, "and I have one to ask."

"I was scairt for a while back that you was fixed to leave me hang on that tree. Guess with all the dead that'll be on this here ground in the next day or two, one more left to die wouldn't of made a whole cart of difference. Would you have left me die?"

"Yes."

"Mister, you are one cold customer. Your pa was right. You got all the feel of a dead toad."

"Come," said Fawn.

"Where to?"

"Are you so happy in this place that you wish to stay?"

"No, I ain't happy in this place. I don't never want to see this hell hole, or them three devils, ever again. Where we going?"

"To the camp of the British on the upper lake. I know where it is and you do not, but I cannot enter the camp. You can. You will be my eyes and my ears inside the camp. All I wish to know is the number of Mohawk that come with you, and will they march with you to attack the fort."

"So you can run and tell the Frenchies?" Ben's voice was hostile.

"No. There is only one Frenchman that I care about, and he is not a soldier. To protect his life, I may need your help if he is taken prisoner."

"So that's the why of it. That there is the reason you saved my neck."

"The only reason."

Eight

Fawn Charbon slept.

The oak in which he lay (his belly tight against a large limb and his arms and legs hanging down on both sides) was close to the British camp. The giant oak grew near a rock ledge, enabling him to climb halfway up and hide in the leaves, even though he was within an arrow shot of the British on the upper lake.

Earlier, before dawn, Fawn had pointed the tree out to Ben. As soon as Ben learned anything he would return to the tree and strike the great trunk with a stick, three times.

And so Fawn waited and slept, silently safe on the arm of the oak. He presumed that on this day, 7 July 1758, the English would move against the French. But he had been wrong. There was the usual clatter of weapons and clank of cookpots below, but no call to arms. No drums. And the Mohawk did not sing of their bravery. Even the bagpipes were silent. General Abercromby was holding his position on the upper lake. Was he considering the loss of his second in command, Brigadier Howe? As he woke, Fawn wondered. The sun was moving west. Had he missed the battle? The thought jolted him awake. For an instant the searing fear of falling made his hands and his body wet.

Fawn was stiff. An oak limb was not the best bed. Yet to sleep so near an army of 15,000 Redcoats and Yengeese was a dare. He felt as a fox must feel when

he eludes wolves. Fawn looked down through the
branches, seeing little but green. Leaves, leaves,
leaves. His legs ached. And he had not eaten for two
days, his insides felt the empty echo of hunger.

Somewhere below, the British cooks were stewing
meat. In his mind, Fawn gulped down the thick bean
porridge, rife with chunks of the orange roots called
carrots . . . and potatoes, the apples of the earth.
And bread! Fawn had once tasted flour bread with
butter on it, a rich taste. There were ovens at the fort,
east of the courtyard. The ovens were underground,
and one of the French soldiers had thrown him a heel
of hot bread. Nearby a woman was working a churn
and she dipped his bread into the cool curds. Straddling the arm of the great oak, Fawn wanted bread
and butter. There were acorns in the oak, but they
were still green and not yet brown and ripe.

Where was Ben?

Would he return, Fawn asked? Yes, he thought, Ben
would return. And if not, there were other ways to
penetrate an English encampment. He recalled the
soldiers in the red coats, as they moved north on the
lake in their boats. They saw nothing, heard nothing.
Old Foot might have walked through their entire
camp and not be seen or heard. Old Foot would see,
and hear. His nose would tell him that behind the
next tree, an Englishman was emptying his bladder.
Or even breathing.

Caution, thought Fawn. It is folly to believe that
the British have no eyes and ears. They have the Mohawk. And it would take only two Mohawk eyes or
two Mohawk ears to discover him.

Fawn wished for Ben to come. Again and again, he
imagined he heard raps on the trunk of the oak. But
instead he heard only the sounds of birds. Then he
heard the bark of a bluejay! But Fawn's ear knew better. It was a noise that no bird would make. A man
had made the call. An instant later, another call. This

one came from a different part of the woods, yet nearby.

Mohawk or Huron?

His body felt the movement way before his ears caught the scraping sound of mocs on oak bark. Some- one was climbing the oak. Someone who thought, as Fawn had thought, that high in this great tree one could view the British camp. Or see those who spied upon it.

Reaching a hand to his back, Fawn's fingers closed on his bow. Then he stopped. On the ground he could run from his kill. But were his foe to scream and drop from his tree, it would not be hard for the fallen man's comrade to discover the source of the arrow. It would be close by, as the leaves were many.

Fawn climbed. I do not, he thought, wish to kill again. The one Huron of last night was one too many, and I am sick with the memory. To kill a man, even to slay a Huron who is about to take the life of a Yen- geese, is poor sport. Old Foot had slain the Huron, but even Old Foot could be wrong. His father, Henri Charbon, had talked to Fawn of these matters. Per- haps it was his gentle father, and not his grandfather, who spoke with wisdom. Somewhere to the north, a Huron woman waits for her man who will never re- turn. Because of me. And yet, the dead Huron himself was a killer and he deserved to die.

Climbing higher, he forced his body through a fork in the trunk. Higher and higher he went in the oak, until his hands were black with bark stain, higher un- til he found the right spot. Here it was, a place to draw his bow, a place where the force of releasing an arrow would not topple him. Fitting the bowstring si- lently into the notch in the arrow's tail, he waited.

Perfect, Fawn thought. Below him was the fork where the one great trunk of the oak became two. When his pursuer reached this spot, his body wedging through the fork, Fawn's arrow would slay him and

yet he would not fall. There will his chest show itself
to receive my arrow, and there will he die. Crows will
come to peck at his eyes.

Close to Fawn's head, a ball of brown leaves was
held by a hand of twigs, the nest of a gray squirrel.
How snug, Fawn thought. A small fort against the
wind of winter. He wanted to part the dry leaves to
see if the squirrels had young, to hear their purr.

His body felt the branches tremble, as if the great
oak itself was afraid, as the climber pushed farther up
the trunk.

Though his own belly was empty, Fawn felt ill with
the sway. He was almost upside down, hanging by his
legs, waiting . . . waiting. He felt the man stop, then
again climb. Each time he stopped, Fawn wondered if
he would climb higher. Each time the man resumed
his upward crawl.

The tree moved sharply.

Had the man fallen? There was no scream. Below,
not far beneath him, branches moved and leaves
told of his upward advance. Fawn pulled back his arrow as the man was about to wedge through the fork
of the trunk that would be his trap and his leafy
grave. Bending his bow, Fawn waited, wondering if
his legs could hold their grip on the tree limbs.

Now he saw a hand! The fingers were open, reaching
up to grasp the branch that farther up held the nest
of the squirrel. The hand took its grip, pulling the
chest into view. Now! But Fawn did not free his arrow.
It was no Mohawk, and not a Huron.

It was Ben.

Nine

"Fawn?"

"Yes. Be still."

"Hey! How come you're away up yonder in them little twigs?"

"Wait there. I will climb down. You were to rap the tree three times. Did you forget our signal?"

"No. But when I was on the rock ledge, I heard a bird call that sounded like it sure didn't come out of no beak."

"I heard it, too. Did you see the Mohawk camp?"

"Sure did. Them Iroquois seem to stay by their lonesomes."

"How many Mohawks?"

"A hundred. Maybe two hundred. Could be a passel more by morning."

Two hundred Mohawk, Fawn thought. Many more than a day ago when he had first seen the Redcoats in the gunboats moving north on Lake George. If the British defeat the French, the Mohawk will demand a share in the victory. But what? Not a French fort. Guns? Perhaps, but possibly more. My guess, Fawn thought, is that the Mohawk want justice. They will want the captured Frenchmen . . . to make sport of, to torture, to kill.

Justice, thought Fawn. A wrong will be righted. Many French Jesuits died, the legend goes, because of the French soldier whose name was Champlain, who killed the Iroquois. Revenge on the Jesuits, Old Foot had said. And now, Fawn swore to himself, the

Frenchman who wounded Old Foot and left him to die may feel the revenge of a Mohawk axe or a Mohawk knife. I hope he dies slowly.

I was a fool to leave my father at the fort. His mind sees nothing but the flag of France, and his bowels wish for nothing but to die in its defense. This must not happen.

"Is the battle tomorrow?" he asked Ben.

"That's what the talk is. General Abercromby don't confide in me much, so I can't say for sure what his plan really is. Hey! What say we climb down? My gut hurts like hell. And all this high living is giving me the vapors."

"If we are not quiet," said Fawn, "you may feel something more deadly than vapors."

"That a fact? Well, we going to spend all summer up here? I say we climb down out of this here old tree, and *eat*."

"Did you bring food?"

"Sure I brung food. You don't think I'd let you starve to bone in a oak tree, after all you done for me. You sliced that old Huron like you been doing it all your life. I guess you Injuns don't mind death."

For an instant, Fawn recalled how his heart had felt, waking that morning not long ago, only to learn that Old Foot would not also awaken. He had touched the dry old hand, like the talon of a fallen eagle, and felt the sting of its coldness. Hard as ice. His father was still asleep. So alone he dragged the thin body of Old Foot to the quiet place beyond LaChute where his mother, Blue Voice, had been buried. With a sharp rock, Fawn had prepared a shallow grave. He lined it with grass, with summer flowers, and tiny white feathers from the wings of a heron. He buried the body along with the hunting bow and three arrows, covering the old warrior with a blanket of fresh green ferns and then a final coverlet of earth. The cold body was no longer his grandfather. Old Foot was now a spirit of the clouds.

"We don't mind death," said Fawn.

"Here," said Ben, reaching a hand inside his shirt. "I got biscuits and a slap of pork and a tin of cold beans. I didn't bother to fetch no plate."

"When a man has not eaten in two days," said Fawn, "he will eat with his hands. Or without. I could eat like a pig, with my snout pushed into a trough of British slop." As he ate, he wondered if his father would be given food at the fort. Yes, because of the deer.

Ben sat astride the great oak limb as if it were a horse, watching Fawn eat. First he ate the biscuits, all four of them. Next, the pork. Then beans.

"How come you saved them beans for last?"

"I am thirsty," said Fawn, "and the meat was salty. But the beans will leave my mouth with a wet taste."

"That makes sense."

"Does your belly hurt?"

"Your darn tootin' it hurts. That big old Huron really stuck me."

"Open your shirt. I will look."

Ben pulled his shirt out of his britches, yanking it up to under his arms to expose his white body.

"The wound is small," said Fawn. "And there is only one."

"One's all it takes, if that's where your heart's hiding. But I sure took the hurt."

"When pain fills the mouth, better to swallow it than to spit out the scream."

"Who said?"

"An old man I once knew," said Fawn.

"Old men say funny words."

"And wise words. But two old men together can often bicker like children."

"You seem old to me, Fawn. How old are you?"

"Sixteen."

"I'm seventeen," said Ben. "I was born in 1741 in the fine old town of Norwich, Connecticut. Where were you born?"

"Here."

"In a oak tree?"

"Yes," said Fawn, pointing to the brown ball of leaves that was the squirrel's nest.

Ben turn to look, and giggled. For a moment he almost lost his balance. He gripped the limb hard with both legs.

"Damn you, Fawn. Laughing hurts my gut."

"Then mark this. Next time you are tree-tied, and a Huron knifes your belly, try not to laugh." Fawn smiled.

"Damn your hide. That's the thanks I git for robbing all that grub for you to eat. But now we're even."

"We are even," said Fawn.

"I don't owe you nothing."

"Nothing. Your life is worth a cut of salty meat, a tin of beans, and four biscuits."

Ben swallowed.

"I get your point. Yeah, I'm beholding to you a bit more than a shirt full of vittles. You name it."

"If the British defeat the French and take prisoners, you will help me take my father from whoever holds him captive, English or Mohawk."

"I was feared you'd say that. It won't be easy. We could both get hung for treason. No, sir . . . it won't be easy."

"A deed worth doing is never easy."

"Who said that, the old man?"

"Another old man. My father."

"He a Mohawk?"

"No. My father is white. He is a man of books, and once he called himself a man of letters. Sometimes when he gets paper from the fort, he makes ink from the crushed husks of butternuts. He writes with a sharpened feather and dusts the wet ink with sand to dry it. He looks to his books for wisdom, and somehow the wisdom of the weasel escapes him. He lives to care for me, and does not know it is the cub who guards the bear. He prays to his God to forgive him, to a God who has no face. My father is a fish who flops on land. We are father and son, yet we are of two tribes."

"But he's still your pa."

"Yes, and I would have no other. He does not know this, and I am sad because I find no words to tell him. He is a man of strong beliefs. As he can no longer live for his belief, it became important for him to die for it. Yet I was a fool to go to the fort, and I was a fool to leave him there. He must not die thinking that I do not see his face. He is all to me, as I am all to him. And if he is taken by the Mohawk, I will trade my life for his."

"Is that all your pa does, just read and write stuff?"

"He also prays, he talks when he is alone, and sometimes goes to the fort to trade our fur for rum. My mother was Mohawk. The winter I was ten, she died of a cough."

"What was your ma like?"

"Soft, yet not afraid. Her name was Blue Voice, daughter of Old Foot. Her leg was crooked and her walk was very slow. She could sing songs about animals and birds. Without her, my father is the autumn tree that has lost its leaves. He was once a Black Robe, a priest. One who will make a prayer for people who cannot make one for themselves. He is clever with thought, clumsy with things."

"He's inside the fort?"

"Yes, because he is French. And as the Mohawk and the British are as many as trees, he went to the fort to be with those who would not let him live as a Frenchman but allow him to die as one."

"Then your father wants General Montcalm to win?"

"As they both are Frenchmen, yes."

"And you?" said Ben.

"I am Mohawk. And the Mohawk side with the Yengeese . . . for now."

"Then you're on the English side."

"I am on Fawn's side. Not the Mohawk side. Not the Yengeese. I see the British and the French make war to decide who will own the land of the Huron and the Mohawk. More than land, they will fight to own all the fish in the water, all the birds in the air. And what will the Mohawk and Huron own? We will chew willow bark like beavers, or fill our bellies with winter wind."

"And if'n the French and British blow each other to bits, us Yankees ain't going to fret. Someday this whole Hudson Valley will not be New England or New France. It'll belong to whoever's man enough to latch on."

"True. So I will not make war under the flag of Britain. A Mohawk who does so cannot see beyond the turtle blood on his face. Let the British die for their king. No Frenchman will take an arrow from Fawn Charbon."

"Is that your name, Fawn? Is it Charbon?"

"Yes. And yours?"

"Mine is Arnold. Benedict Arnold."

Ten

The mud on his body was cold, making his spine dance.

Lying in the swamp, Fawn had waited for darkness and slowly the dark had come. Moment by moment, the distant babble of many Mohawk voices became smothered by the voices of insects. Only his face and ears were above the black water, listening. The bay water was shallow, no deeper than half an arrow, and more earth than water.

He listened to the Mohawk speak among themselves. Two Crows, a man who did much of the talking, said that at the next sunrise the British would win a great victory over their enemies, the French. And the Mohawk would share in the victory. Other voices grunted agreement, but not all. Another voice said it would be wise to let the Yengeese kill the French and the Huron. Two Crows answered by saying that then there would be little of the victory for the Mohawk. No guns, no tobacco, no French prisoners. To share in the triumph, the Mohawk must first redden their hatchets.

Two Crows then sang of past victories over the Huron and how his father had told him of driving the Huron back into the cold of the north, the place called Canada. The song said that many Huron women were now alone because of the bravery of the Mohawk warrior and his skill with the bow. And finally the singing of Two Crows became lost in the singing of bugs.

The song of Two Crows did not leave Fawn's ear.

He kept hearing over and over the Mohawk's desire to kill Frenchmen. I was a fool, he thought, to leave my father at the fort. A fool! But would he have done other than stay? No, so there he is. Ah, the times he has gone sleepless worrying about me, and now it is the fawn who frets for the safety of the old stag. What can I do now, go to the fort and ask him to come with me? No, he will stay as he now wishes to fight for France. Nor would I even reach the fort in this darkness; for on this night the French sentries will be many and a bald Mohawk who is Fawn Charbon would make a fine target.

The time is tomorrow, after the battle. Or during. Yes, tomorrow I go to my father. Perhaps once he has seen the might of Abercromby's army or hears reports of its size, his senses will return and together we will go north and let soldiers slay soldiers.

Fawn still did not move. Near his face, a large cow-frog poked her head up through the black blanket of water and weeds. Her throat expanded and belched out a roaring croak. The throat was expanding to croak again, but the second croak never came. Fawn's hand shot forward, quick as the tongue of a snake, and the frog would be his supper. He would eat it raw.

Crawling slowly through the muddy water, Fawn left the swamp that was east of the Mohawk camp, crossing LaChute to wash himself clean. To the west, British campfires were everywhere. Soldiers prepared meals, cleaned weapons, and shouted to each other in English. Carrying the big frog, Fawn circled behind the British encampment, heading for the oak tree. Early this morning, Ben had rejoined his fellow colonials, but said he would return to the tree as soon as it was dark.

Looking at a British campfire, Fawn longed to be near. Buckskin and body, he was cold and wet. Yet he dared not build a fire, at least not until he found Ben.

A noise was behind him! Fawn's body was rigid as his hand moved slowly to his hip, only to discover a bitter fact. His knife was missing. Quietly, he released the cowfrog, allowing his supper to escape.

The sound came again. A rustling of leaves, as if the creator of the noise cared not who heard. No Mohawk would so move, and no Huron. It was a white man, or a white boy. Ben? Fawn lay still. He would not be so unwise as to meet the sound. He would let the sound move to him. Old Foot had said that when you do not know where to run, do not run at all. The sound came again, but no closer. To Fawn's ear it told no story, except that whatever it was could not come to him. It was trapped. And now he felt he could move with less danger.

The rabbit kicked the night air.

Someone, Fawn did not know who, had set the snare. The loop was tightening around the rabbit's neck, tighter with every kick. The thin sapling had whipped erect, and the rabbit danced his last dance among the small black leaves. By the time Fawn reached the snare, the rabbit had strangled. It would never kick again.

Fawn Charbon was hungry and the rabbit would be food. Old Foot had been with him when he had snared his first rabbit. The old man had yanked off the white puff of a tail and teased his chin. Old Foot said to wait two suns before eating it, for the meat to cool and cure. But now, Fawn Charbon was too hungry to wait. It was a long walk down to the fort below, too dark, and there were too many Huron. He needed salt. Soaking the dead rabbit all night in cold water and salt would help to prepare the meat, and to drive out the sickness of death. And in the dark he dared not risk a fire.

Everywhere in the darkness, men shouted in Yengeese. Some spoke as his father sometimes spoke, in soft English words. Others, the colonials, talked through their noses, as did Ben. Listening, Fawn stroked the fur of the dead rabbit. It was still warm. The stiffness of death had not yet come.

Staying low to the ground, moving silently through the thick forest, Fawn worked his way south toward the big oak that would (he sighed) have to be his bed for a second night. The oak was their private meeting place, his and Ben's. He wondered if Ben had the same thought. Perhaps not. Ben's face and heart were open and no doubt he had many friends in the Yengeese camp. But in the boats, the men were common. Boys were few. As he approached the oak tree, carrying the dead rabbit, he heard . . .

"Fawn."

Looking up in the darkness, he saw Ben straddling the first limb of the oak. Ben's back leaned against the bumpy trunk and a gun rested crosswise on the branch. His legs hung down. Ben had wanted to see him again, and the thought of it almost made Fawn forget all else. "I was hoping you'd come," Ben whispered.

"And I hoped you would also come."

"Here! I'll toss ya my gunpiece so's I can snake down out'n this here wood."

Dropping the rabbit, Fawn caught the gun with both hands. It was heavy. As heavy, Fawn thought as he watched Ben climb down from the cliff that was close to the tree trunk, as a hundred arrows.

"This is the first time that I hold a gun," he said to Ben. "Did you make it?"

Ben laughed. "Me, make that? Shucks, no. My old man's a soldier and he says that a musket, which is what that there is, was invented by some Italian with the name of Moschetta. So maybe *he* made the durn thing."

"Is it a good gun?"

"Wouldn't know. I never got close enough to the Frenchies to hardly snap the cock."

"But you were with Lord Howe," said Fawn.

"Yeah, but I don't guess I saw much. What in hell could a man see in all them trees? This ain't a battle-field. It's a cussed woodpile. And *our* boys, we wasn't even a flash in the pan. None of us colonials knew where in all suffering we was, and you can't tell me the British did either. Someone even took a shot at Major Rogers. Can you imagine a tomfool thing like that? Why, I druther face old Mister Montcalm with my bare fists than fall into a shoot-out with Robert Rogers. They say his daddy was an injun and his mother was a bear, so he got born with a temper that even Hell won't have."

"I have not seen Hell, but my father says there is such a place . . . a place we make with our own hands."

"Yeah? Well, reckon I'll see the Hot Place soon enough. What's the rabbit for?"

"To eat. The rabbit is still warm with life and needs salt."

"Be right back," said Ben. In no longer than a man could hold his breath five times, Ben returned carrying a small white bag.

"Here," he said, handing the bag to Fawn. His hands were white with salt. "A present to you from George."

"George?"

"That old cottontail rabbit o' yourn will never know it, but he's about to stew in the King's salt. I don't guess King George will know it either, so it puts your supper and Old George in the same sauce."

Fawn smiled.

With Ben it was like a hunt with Old Foot. Ben talked in pictures; and in his mind, Fawn could see a rabbit and the king as they bubbled in a pot. Suddenly, suddenly, suddenly his belly leaped with hunger. He and Ben would eat supper. Together they would talk, sharing food and friendship. For this, he would risk a fire.

Fawn's hand reached for his knife. But the small

deerhide sheath was empty and flat. He had no knife. But now it did not matter. The knife that he had lost was small. He would make another, or ask his father to trade for a knife at the fort, and the new one would be long, like the knife of Old Foot.

"You ain't got a knife," said Ben, "so how you aim to undress that there animal?"

"Without a knife," said Fawn.

His fists tight together, Fawn held a hind leg of the rabbit near his chest. He ripped his hands apart, and the skin tore evenly all around the joint. Fawn did the same with the other hind leg. Running a finger up under the trouser of skin, he tore the hide to the crotch.

"Hold the back feet," he said to Ben.

With Ben's help, the skin peeled downward toward the head. Fists together again, he broke the skin at the first joints of the front paws. He ripped up each shoulder with a finger and the skin came free except for the head. With a quick twist, Fawn broke the neck; the head and skin came cleanly off.

"I'll be dumped," said Ben. There was respect in his voice and Fawn felt himself fed by it. It was not food, but yet it filled like food.

"I will teach you to do this," said Fawn.

"You already have. Looks like that there rabbit is wearing fur mittens." It was true. The rabbit was now without fur, except for its four paws.

Fawn tossed the head and hide into the bushes. He put the rabbit on its back on a rock. Finding a sharp stone, he made a long cut from the throat to the crotch. With a deeper jab, he split the breast bone and the pelvic bone. Then he slashed the inside of each rear leg. Now it was easy to gut.

With rocks, they made a small tub in the edge of the lake to contain the washed rabbit, clean water and the bag of salt. Fawn saved a handful of salt, some of which he ate. Waiting for the rabbit to soak in the brine water, they talked in whispers.

Ben said, "Captain Carter wants to pull out now. He says, far as he's concerned, us colonials ain't fixing to take even one more shot at Monsieur Montcalm. He says the next soul he shoots will be old Abercromby. Some of our men already up and left disgusted. Captain says deserters oughta get shot. He said he'd shoot me, too . . . if I weren't such a damn curiosity. As for me, all I want to do is hightail it back to civilization and smell a fresh haircut. This whole durn expedition is nothin' but a wild goose chase. A flash in the pan. All I see is them Scottish getting ready to go down the hill with their pipes wailing like witches. All us colonials will be in the rear guard."

"You saw a battle," said Fawn.

"A small battle."

"Fawn Charbon will not be a soldier, if this is what soldiers do. Wait to kill and then kill."

"You killed that Huron who had me hogtied to a tree. You put an arrow through his neck like it was your steady line of work."

"My arrow killed the Huron to help save the life of my father, by saving you. Not to kill the Huron."

"Where is your father? Still at the fort?"

"Yes, at the fort. But I wish he were in France, for when he sleeps he is there."

"Never thought I'd say it," said Ben, "but the idea of home sure is appealing. I'd give a corporal's pay just to see my sister walk out to the milk house, and lift a scum of cream with her fingers and mix it with a hot batch of green peas. You like peas?"

"Yes," said Fawn, wondering what *peas* was and how it tasted.

"How come you and them blue eyes stare at me thataway?" said Ben.

"I ask myself if you have many friends, Ben Arnold."

"Yeah, I got friends back home. You got friends?"

"I have one," said Fawn.

Eleven

"That's a poorly fire," said Ben.

"Meat does not cook when the flame is high."

"Well if it don't cook, what *does* it do?"

"It burns," said Fawn. "The outside crust will be black, but the heart of the meat will be red and raw."

Rolling it between his brown hands, Fawn twisted the spit stick that held the rabbit. The far end of the stick rested in the crotch of a short fork-branch. Fawn added another twig to the orange nest of heat.

"You been cooking that there animal for most an hour. Smells so good it's giving my gut the gumptions. I ain't ett since noon."

"I have eaten once in three days," said Fawn.

"Then how come you can set there and spin that stick and stay sane?"

"Because the meat is raw. My grandfather said that hunger in watching makes meat taste better. He called it the gravy of patience."

"What was he, some sort of poet?"

"He was a Mohawk," said Fawn.

"What was his name?"

"Old Foot."

"That name could make a dog laugh," said Ben.

"So could Benedict."

"I been in a passel of fistfights about that. You ever been in a fight?"

"No. I know only my parents and my grandfather. Now, only my father. We were four with much land, so there was no reason to fight. But now many men .

come. The French from the north and the British from the south. Neither think they own enough land, and there will be much war."

"How come you say that?" said Ben.

"Land is what things fight for. All things."

"You mean that's what people want."

"Not just people. It is what the tree wants with its roots. Its leaves want the land of the sky and a small flower aches with the same want. So does the spider in her web and the ant in her hole. So if you are a soldier, you will fight more for land than for your name."

"You're a spook, you know that," said Ben.

"I am already so many things, being one more matters little. But now let us decide if Fawn Charbon is a cook."

"You'll burn your fingers on that meat."

"A hungry hand feels no pain from hot food."

They ate the rabbit. In the darkness, biting beneath the black crust, the creamy meat steamed wet and fresh. They ate until the mouth of each boy was ringed with black. Salt made the cooking taste even sharper, as once again the rabbit was served by King George of England. Above their heads, attracted by the firelight, a storm of white moths flew about like summer snow.

"Too bad we have no rum," said Ben.

"There are better drinks than rum."

"Like what?"

"Tea."

"Be right back," said Ben.

He was, carrying a small tin of tea and a handful of sugar. The sugar sifted down through his fingers; and as it landed, even the fire seemed excited. Fawn had folded a bark pot, boiled water; and the two of them drank the strong hot tea, sweet with sugar, from the same birch cup.

"Land," said Ben, wiping his mouth on his sleeve. "You got a point, Fawn. And I been studying on it for

some time. Fact is, I don't give a rat's ass who wins
this here war . . . so long as England and France
tucker themselves all out doing it, and the winner is
panting like a dog in August."

"I see two hawks," said Fawn, "who fight in the sky
until one drops a mouse, which falls to the beak of a
crow."

"Is that how you see England and France, as a pair
of hawks who drop a mouse?"

"Yes. I care not who wins."

"That," said Ben, "puts you an' me on the same
side."

"No," said Fawn.

"How come?"

"Yankee is the crow, and Mohawk is the mouse."

"Well put," said Ben. "And so I say to you, friend
Fawn, the mouse must become the crow. For you,
Mister Charbon, that oughta be a Sunday cinch, seeing
as you be half crow and half mouse."

"In a forest of owls," said Fawn, "mice are spat out
as broken bones and fur."

"Someday," said Ben, "you won't see a British flag
in this valley. Not one. And what a valley it is. I don't
guess I seen even half of it. We come up the Hudson
River, then overland to Fort William Henry. What a
river! What a piece of property. What a fee for a man
to hold."

"One man can own a river?" said Fawn.

"Yes, sir," said Ben. "You bet your boots he can."

"I have no boots."

"What I mean is, when you pick a thumb of land
that commands a waterway . . ."

"The way the French built Fort Carillon?"

"Yes," said Ben. "I seen that true on a map. And
same thing is true for the Hudson. A fort! Just one fort
could tame it all. One man could command all the
farmland, and make the Dutchies pay tribute in gold
and produce. That is, if they want their harvest barges
to pass under my guns."

"And you will build the fort and own it all?"

"I will own it all. And the water will be the River Arnold. But that's only a start. We could change the course of the river, or dig a canal, so a barge could float from New York to Canada."

"Canada is a land of French and Huron, and the great white bear."

"Only for now. The British will push north. Monsieur Montcalm would be on his way north right now, with his tail feathers on fire, if'n Lord Howe hadn't of got hisself leaded. Yeah, the Redcoats'll push them Frenchies clear up to Hudson Bay. And that'll be just the start of George's trouble. Old George of England will have more land than he can defend or farm."

"That is when Ben Arnold will take it?"

"Yes. Land belongs to soldiers, not farmers. The farmers work it, but soldiers own it."

"Were I a farmer, Ben Arnold would not take what is mine."

"What *is* yours? Just so's I don't make that mistake."

"This bow. These three arrows. My father and I own a house north of the fort. It is on the high ground near where the French cut down all the trees, and where the fort looks north to Canada. My father owns some books. And he owns an axe head. It was a gift to him from Old Foot. Without the axe, my father said to me when I was small, we could not have built the house."

"I live in a white house, back in Connecticut. Is your house white? Reckon not."

"It is of the forest, made of bark and very snug. My father and grandfather built it when I was born. The floor and the beds are straw. It has a cooking pit for a fire, and a hole in the roof to free the smoke."

"And that's where you learned all this stuff, the way you speak French and Mohawk . . . and English, good as one of them British nobles. Good as Lord Howe. Your old man taught it?"

"Yes. He learned from a man who was his teacher in

France. His name was Brother Anthony. My father speaks to many people in their own tongue. My father knows much, for he is a learned man. Two Waters is no place for a scholar. And no place for Fawn Charbon."

"You don't aim to stay?" said Ben.

"The day my father dies, I leave. He is old, like a flower that has dried in the sun and yet it still stands. I believe he will die soon, and I cannot let him die without his son to cross hands. When the sky opens for Henri Charbon, only then will a new land open for Fawn. I owe my father much. His cloud must be pink, and not a black cloud that is heavy with a rain of tears."

"Fawn?"

"Yes."

"How would you like to come to Connecticut? After your pa dies."

"And be a druggist?"

"No. I ain't about to be no druggist. I tried, but I weren't even a flash in the pan. Only thing I learned about chemistry was how to make gunpowder. It's mostly saltpeter. Three-quarters of it is. The rest of it's in five parts; three charcoal and two sulphur."

"Yes. I would like to come to Connecticut. I want to see many places."

"My sister would like you. She likes wild things. You'd like her, too. Sis is a good old gal. She's the *real* soldier of the family. Oughta see her shoot a squirrel."

Fawn was quiet for a while, thinking about all that Ben had said. Some of which made sense, some a mystery.

"Ben, what is a flash in the pan?"

"Here. It's a place in the firing part of a musket. A flash means a failure, and it's when the primer goes off and not the main charge."

"Perhaps that is what I will be in Connecticut."

"Fawn, I only know you a day. But I tell you true. If'n there's one thing you *ain't*, it's a flash in the pan."

The fire was between them as they lay on their backs; hands under heads, using their fingers for pillows. As a stick shifted in the fire, sparks went up rising like a frightened flock of small yellow birds into a dark summer sky.

"Fly," said Fawn. "Fly to make stars."

Twelve

"It will be light soon," said the French soldier.

"Yes," said Henri.

"Perhaps they will come."

"The British will come, my son. Only to learn a bitter lesson, that you and your comrades await them. Your general has not been idle. Our outer lines bristle with fallen trees."

"General Montcalm came to our barracks in the night. He said he could not sleep. Hardly any of us could sleep. He asked us young ones if we were afraid. We all said no, trying to look very brave."

"You *are* brave," said Henri.

"I hope to be. General Montcalm said that he had been afraid on nights before a battle. It was hard to believe. He always looks so . . . so . . ."

"So sure."

"Yes," said the soldier. "He sat with us, and drank a dram of rum at our side. And he told us the truth."

"What did he tell you?"

"I asked if it were true, were there fifteen thousand English soldiers to our three thousand? He said it was true. Then he said it means that I must shoot only five. We all laughed."

"He is an able commandant."

"That is true. If only the three thousand of us were as noble as he."

"You will be, lad."

Standing on the stone of the high gray wall of Fort Carillon, Henri Charbon squinted into the foggy blackness; looking north and west, past the clearing, toward the place that had been his home for seventeen years. How had they managed to survive? Seventeen winters, sometimes with weeks of bitter cold, when LaChute was a giant white feather of ice, and the frozen spike of wind stabbed through their furs and into their very souls.

Blue Voice could make fire. Luckily, for he and Blue Voice spent their first winter alone in a cave, seeing no one else. But there were often moc tracks in the snow. Yet they heard no one. Sometimes meat was left hanging at the cave's mouth: a rabbit, a brace of gray squirrels, and once a young doe. In the spring, sometimes fish. All had been killed by Old Foot, he later learned. The warrior had not wished for his crippled daughter and her French mate to starve.

A baby was born to Blue Voice.

This time Old Foot came to the cave, hearing the yelps of his grandchild, and wishing to see this strange fruit with his own eyes. Old Foot held the babe in his arms, high in the air. "Fawn," he had said in English. The name stuck. And now there was no keeping Old Foot away. On his next visit he brought Henri a gift, the head of an axe. Together, he and Old Foot built the tiny house of bark. Old Foot insisted that it have two rooms, and Henri did not guess that the old man wanted the second room for himself. A guest room, for a permanent guest.

Every waking moment, Old Foot spent with the baby. He made a cradle of pine boughs, with a soft interior of white egret feathers. He made a rattle of beaver bone. For hours he danced, holding the baby in his arms. Sometimes he sang softly. At night, he and Fawn occupied the second room. And in the winter they slept as close as two spoons.

As Fawn grew up, Old Foot grew old. Yet the bond between them made the grandfather and grandson like bark and tree. When Fawn was ten, Blue Voice died of congestion of the chest . . . and Old Foot did not weep. Nor would he permit Fawn to weep. Looking at his lifeless mother, the boy had started to cry. Old Foot beat him with a stick. I remember, thought Henri. On that day, I remember how I leaped at Old Foot, knocking him to the ground. And before my heart could beat even one more beat, an arrow was drawn in his bow, its point toward my chest. The look in Old Foot's eye as he drew his bowstring said it all. A look of hatred. Suddenly Henri was no longer the father of the coveted grandchild. Henri was an unnecessary Frenchman, Old Foot was thinking, and the French were made to die by a Mohawk arrow. Had it not been for that ten-year-old boy who hurled his taut little body at his grandfather, I would be dead. Henri saw the look in the face of Old Foot, whose intention was to kill. The sound he made in his throat was not human, more like the sound of a captured wolf Henri had seen in Canada.

Henri had faced Old Foot, even though the Mohawk's bow was still drawn. It had been then that Henri had said in English, a language that Old Foot understood, "Beat my son again, for any reason, and I will kill you."

Slowly, Old Foot relaxed his bow, throwing it over his shoulder. Quickly, with a snap of his hands, he broke the arrow's back, handing half of it to Henri. "Black Robe," he had said, "you not rabbit."

"Look," said the young soldier, bringing Henri back from the past, back to a wall of a fort where he searched the darkness to see his child.

"Where?"

"Behind you, sir. The sun!"

Turning himself about, Henri looked across Lake Champlain and up to the rim of the green mountains to the east. There was no sun. But a long gray streak lay atop the high ridge, growing longer.

"It grows long, like a great white snake," the soldier said.

"Yes," said Henri, "it does."

"I wonder," said the boy, "if I shall ever see another dawn."

"There are British soldiers who see that same sun, and ask the same question. Boys who long for the English Midlands just as you long for France. How old are you?"

"I'm eighteen," said the soldier. "I ran away from home to enlist. What a fool I was."

"Perhaps not. We all run from something. I too ran away."

"You did?"

"Yes. I ran away from my Church, my faith, and my duty. Worse yet, on this night I ask myself, have I run away from my own son?"

"I ran away from a farm. My father is a farmer," said the soldier. "Right about now, he's going to the barn for milking. We have six cows. I can even smell the damp straw. I can hear the hot milk ring the bucket. Like a bell."

The soldier pumped his fist several times, as if his hand were working the udder of his father's cow, a cow that was an ocean to the east.

"But you chose to be a French soldier," said Henri, "and just think. One day you shall retire with honor and milk all the cows you wish."

The boy was weeping. Hidng his face so Henri would not see.

"Easy, my son. Your life is not yet ended. I, too, have been afraid. Seventeen years ago, up beyond those hills, I was once so very afraid. I was alone, with no comrades to soldier at my side. And no general to steady my hand. So don't cry, my son. Don't let the British hear you cry."

The young soldier wiped his face with the sleeve of his uniform. His eyes were hidden in the shadows, and Henri was grateful that the night offered the boy some privacy for his shame.

"You are not a coward," he said to the boy. "We all weep when we think of home. Back in those trees, a young boy in a red coat, whose name you and I shall never learn, weeps for England. And he wonders if he shall ever see his bonnie little island again."

"I was fine," said the soldier, "until I remembered it was milking time. I raised one of our cows all by myself, up from a calf. She's brown and white. A real beauty she is, proud and fair. Her name is Eugenie."

"Eugenie? What a fine name for a cow!"

"Listen!"

Henri was still. Then he said, "I hear nothing."

"Listen," the boy said again. "Don't you hear? It comes from up there. Like insects around a barn at midday. Hear it?"

Henri closed his eyes, and heard. They were still a long way off, but each step brought the sound closer. The pipes! A thousand bagpipes from behind the blackness of a thousand trees, and not one would be seen. Had the general forgotten to tell the men about the pipes? The British would not advance unless they bore the sting of Scottish bees.

"Spirits," said the young soldier.

"No, my son."

"Ghosts. Ghosts, I say. No living thing makes a wail like that. No living creature."

"It is only bagpipes in a morning mist."

"Why don't the infernal British come bearing arms, and fight like men? No, like sirens they come. Like the tale my grandmother told of the evil sisters, who could burn a mark on an unborn child. I had a cousin that bore a witch pox. The poor soul went mad before she was weaned."

"They filled your head, boy."

"Hear, then."

"It is only Scottish music. And those who make it are soldiers, not evil hags."

"Like the chants of a wake. A spirit is caught between this world and the next, they say. Look there! I see one."

WHAM!

The young soldier fired his musket at an unseen note, at a piper who blew the note high on the west hill, beyond the reach of cannon. Trying to reload, the boy was shaking. Placing both his hands on the boy's face, Henri forced the lad to look at him.

"Soldiers, boy. Not ghosts. Soldiers so far away they beg for your lead. Nothing will please them more than to hear you discharge your arms at a shadow. Be steadfast. There's not one Englishman in range. Here we are, safe on the fort wall. And out there, no Englishman has even reached our mighty row of fallen trees."

"Can't you hear it, sir? The sound?"

"Yes, I hear it. Strange, but not evil. Imagine yourself as a city boy. You have never ever seen a cow. And in the dark of early morn you hear Eugenie plead to be milked. Imagine how false, how silly your fear would be."

"A cow is something else, sir."

"Yes, but to a virgin ear, a bag of milk can be as chilling as a bag of music."

"I must reload. They'll come, and I will not have poured the powder or put a ram to the barrel."

The boy's body was trembling. He dropped his powder tin on the stone battlement, causing a clatter. Throwing down his musket, he fell to his knees. His head was bowed.

"I'm going to die, Father. Hear my confession, please."

Now the young soldier was looking up at Henri; his eyes were pleading, begging, crying for absolution. And there was no way for Henri to offer it.

"I cannot, my son. I am not a priest."

"Yes, sir, you are. I've heard the talk, like they say. The whole garrison knows. You're a priest. You're a priest! You're a . . ."

Henri's hand cupped the boy's mouth. Going down also on his own knees, Henri held the boy in his arms. The young body seemed so frail. A toy of war, he thought. If only this were my own child I hold in my arms. If only he were Fawn.

"Bless me, Father. The evil pipes will curse my soul and drive me mad if you do not hear my confession."

As the boy clawed his own ears with his fingers, Henri Charbon drew back his hand and with a wide swing, he slapped the face of the soldier as hard as he could.

"Don't let the pipes drive you mad, my son. For that is exactly their purpose. Know only this, that the men who play those pipes have no more courage than you and I."

The boy was still. Stone still, as if the stinging slap had been a blessing from his God.

"Thank you," he said. "Father."

Thirteen

The sudden but distant sound of bagpipes made Fawn's head jump up from the rough limb of the oak which had, for a second night, been his bed. In the time of a heartbeat, he remembered where he was, and why.

Looking down, the earth and the many leaves below were black and still. But above, toward the gray sky, high in the lacy crown of the great tree, gold began to dance with a single leaf. Then another and another. Or did the leaves tremble as they heard the British pipe their song of war through the forest? What was today? He had lost the track of time. As his head cleared away the thick cloud of sleep, he remembered.

It was 8 July 1758. His father had told him always to know what day it is, for "that is our lanyard to a civil world."

What a noise! No telling from where it came, Fawn thought. The bagpipes were here, over there, above and below. They seemed to march upon the wind. It made the flesh slink along his spine, as if to hide from the wail. None were near, Fawn concluded. So either late last evening, or before sunrise, the British had advanced through the black woods, down the portage path toward Fort Carillon.

Moments later, Fawn Charbon was down from his oak, rummaging near the edge of the British encampment. He found meat, apples, cheese and bread. He ate hurriedly. If the battle was on this day, he must see. Leaving the camp, he saw a partly drunk bottle of rum. He tasted it. The taste was foul, but it added fire to his belly. His father had made him drink rum once, forcing it down his throat after a day when the two of them had gathered firewood in the snow for hours. Then he had reminded his father how Old Foot had called rum "the hot medicine."

"Medicine for many ills," Henri had said, but he did not smile as he drank.

Below the abandoned camp of the British, Fawn saw signs of where many of the Mohawk had been. Bending close to the ground, he smelled a Mohawk smell on a circle of flattened grass, where one of the scouts had slept. It was a strong smell, like the cave of a bear. Nearby, in a bush, was a discarded moc along with small strips of fresher deerskin. The warrior had stopped here to sleep and to replace the worn moccasin with a fresh one, cut from the flaps of hide that covered his loins.

Leaving the upper lake, Fawn trotted east through the wet smoke of morning, moving in the mist toward the rising sun, down toward the lower lake and Fort Carillon. The bugs of night had stilled their song, but the birds of morning had not begun theirs. They know, Fawn thought. A choir of sparrows scolded him as he passed silently beneath their tree, causing him to think of the battle. Sparrows, he said wordlessly to the forest roof, you will soon be disturbed by more than Fawn.

High above the fort to the west, a rock ledge provided a wide view of the British advance. It was a living map, Fawn thought. He could see three columns of advancing Redcoats—the Scottish Highlanders of the Black Watch, according to Ben. Behind them in a curved line was a rear guard of more British regulars, followed by the colonials of New Jersey and Connecticut. Somewhere down there was Ben Arnold, Fawn thought, on his way to being a soldier instead of . . . what was it? . . . yes, a druggist.

Wedging his body snugly between two gray rocks, Fawn saw more. A troop of men in buckskin carried long rifles with no knives on the end. Rangers, according to Ben's description, under the command of Robert Rogers.

The Ranger advance was not the same as the Redcoats. The British moved through the brush, bending the green bushes or breaking them. The Rangers move as the soft wind moves, Fawn thought, as water runs through the fingers. As the Rangers moved, the forest around them did not. Ben had said how much he had admired their leader, Major Rogers.

Nowhere could Fawn see any sign of the Mohawk. Two Crows and his warriors had become smoke.

As the morning light grew stronger, the mist began to melt into day. Looking east, Fawn could see the great gray star of stone that was Fort Carillon. How well he remembered, years ago, when the French soldiers had come south in many boats. The point at Ticonderoga, where LaChute (the waters of Lake George) calmly poured into Lake Champlain, had been nothing but woodland. Tree after tree had felt the axe. Rock by rock, the French engineers and their oxen began to build the fortress. Day by day and year by year, the big star was built. The cannon came, the huge balls of iron; barrel after barrel of black powder, and mortars, and men. Along came wives and children, horses and cows, sheep and goats and pigs, the noise and the smell.

Now, thought Fawn, on this one day, all will flee or be destroyed. The British army of Genral Abercromby will drive the French and their stinking cookpots north to Canada. But then the British will stay. The evening air will be foul with Scottish pipes. Fawn, he told himself, you trade one tribe of white devils for another. For everywhere a white foot walks, the ground is dust instead of grass. Water is foul where white bodies swim. Deer once came to drink from the lower lake at the point of land where the fort now stands. But now the deer no longer come. And the otter who once splashed below the white water of La-Chute are gone. Also the beaver.

I would trade, Fawn thought, all the French and British soldiers to once again hear one slap of a beaver's tail. Or hear his whistle.

The sun was up now, but its warmth would not quickly bake the gray cold of the rock. Fawn had a cramp in his leg, but he did not choose to move freely in the light of morning. Old Foot has once advised him always to travel in darkness, for the day was a time of stillness. So Fawn did not move. He lay quietly, the hard grit of rock against his face, listening to the bees of the British. The pipes played on and on and on, driving sting after sting into French courage.

I have begun, Fawn thought, to live in such careless ways. I eat the white man's food and laugh in the trees with Ben. I move to this open ledge of rock with more wonder than purpose. Now is time for thought, for never have I seen so many soldiers. Could there be any doubt as to the battle's outcome? I wonder about the count in the French garrison. My father had said three thousand. I saw five times as many British on the upper lake, and heard the voices of many Mohawk.

Five to one. The British will win a great victory. The French will surrender their stronghold. And the Mohawk will sing with joy in their rapturous slaughter of the Huron. Old Foot would have enjoyed this day, to even the score against Monsieur Champlain.

The pipes stopped. Everything was silent, and the birds in the treetops respected the stillness as they had the noise. The advance through the trees had come to a halt. What was old General Abercromby up to now? And how, Fawn wondered, did the sudden quiet strike into the ear of the great Montcalm?

How dull I am, Fawn though, to think about generals when my father is in peril. It is Henri Charbon who may rot in the fort's dungeon or a British prison.

Or worse, the victorious English could throw him, like
a ball to be played with, to the Mohawk and their
sport, men who spoke as had Two Crows.

Has my father come so far from his home in France,
Fawn thought, for such an end? He came as a Black
Robe, in peace, without weapons. So let him live in
peace, and die in peace. My father, Fawn thought,
was the man who came to the lake of the Mohawk . . .
alone. And he became the only Frenchman that Old
Foot would not slay. Seventeen winters, he kept us,
with the help of Old Foot. Yet as our fires burned out,
so did he.

Three days, Fawn remembered. For three days, one
winter, his father had gone north alone to the French
fort at Saint Frédéric to beg for food. Three days and
three nights of walking through snow, following the
west bank of Lake Champlain. Old Foot was sick. I
was only a child. Blue Voice had to stay with us,
which left only my father to go forty miles through
the cold and empty white. Old Foot said my father
would not return. I said he would. And he did return,
with rum, meat, medicine, a sack of beans . . . and a
book. A book! Fawn smiled, remembering how his father had read and reread that very book, the one that
had been written by an Englishman called Bacon.
Twenty miles through snow with a book. How ill. And
yet, how true to his character and his dreams.

But the illness of my father's mind this day, thought
Fawn, is worry for his son. But how can I rest the
mind of my father, and take him from the fort into the
forests where no Redcoat and no Mohawk will find
us? Why was I so blind? I had seen the might of the
Yengeese in their countless boats. Yet I took my father
to the fort. And there he stays, like a fly in a bottle.

There he frets. I imagine his thoughts are more of
my safety than his own. Still he worries, not knowing
that the home of his pup is the forest and not in a fort.
Here I am free, as a cloud is free in the sky and a bird
in wing. As the bat is at liberty to flee her cave at

first light and again at dusk. He told me once, Fawn thought, of the seaman he knew who kept a bird in cage. A parrot, a bird whose feathers had much color, he said. Yet I believe there was little color in its heart, and little joy in its confinement.

Were I now with my father, *safe* in his stone cage of Frenchmen, does he not know how the color would drain from Fawn, the red from my skin and the blue from my eye, until my spirit is as gray as the fort.

He does not know me, this man who is my father. He knows only himself and his books that were written by fools who were strangers to the law. He talks of his mighty King of Nazareth who was a carpenter, and of his friend who was Peter the Fisher and who was also a rock. How my father longs to live as they lived, yet he wishes neither to build nor fish. He talked often of the carpenter called Jesus, and the words that he had spoken. More blessed to give than to receive, he once read to us. If ever a thought was an illness, it is that. Does the squirrel give away her store of nuts? Would a bird yield a captured worm, or the bee her honey? My father asks LaChute to flow uphill. I have tried to understand his words; but inside I laugh, as Old Foot and Blue Voice laughed. We laughed until we saw the hurt in his eyes, as he knew pain because we did not understand all the stories he told us of his carpenter, the one who said that the meek are blessed.

Perhaps so, but mostly the meek are eaten.

My father called Old Foot an animal, as if an animal were a scrap of dirt. If we wish to see dirt, or to smell it, we have only to mark the French slop that spills from the fort's cookhouse. No animal has ever left such a scar to the nose or eye. So if such is man, then Fawn Charbon is an animal. I walk with wolves. And this is what my father does not understand.

Old Foot once said that there can be two blades to a knife. How well does Fawn Charbon understand his father? Do I so mourn the coldness of Old Foot that

my ear is deaf to the living heartbeat of my old
Frenchman? I felt the pain of the forkhorn, yet not
the pain of Henri Charbon. Once he was young and
straight, a man who faced Mohawk warriors, strong as
a tree . . . before the chill of being a lone white man
bent his trunk, and stripped him of bark and spirit.

When he sired me his seed was strong; for I am
whole, and not crippled like my mother. He was oak.
Now, he is an oak too old to blossom with acorns. So I
will allow no British piper to cut him down. And there
will be no Mohawk to kick his belly, or burn his flesh.

Brave talk. But how can I reach the fort now? Redcoats will soon cover it as flies blacken a dead salmon.

The ditch!

Fawn remembered the drainage ditch that carried
slop water from the fort down to the mouth of La-
Chute. A foul ditch of evil smells, but a way in and a
way out. If I know my father, he will walk the wall
that looks north and west, toward our home. The
ditch enters the fort there, and that is where I will
drag the fly from the spider's web.

My father will not wish to come. But once he sees
the swarm of British, and by now he has heard the
wail of their pipes, he may harken to reason. Together
we will go north, to a place where British do not
slaughter French and where the Mohawk do not slay
the Huron. If there is such a place.

I go to the fort. Now, before the battle. With so
many handsome red uniforms to see, who will see
Fawn? He will move as the worm moves. I will be
mud that crawls through mud.

Fourteen

The water was cold. But it was his only route.

At times, Old Foot had said, the easiest thing to see escapes all eyes. To all who saw that morning of 8 July 1758, it was no more than a small round hemlock bush (no bigger than a barrel) that floated down the fast waters of LaChute. Many men were about that morning. Three thousand pairs of French eyes squinted westward to detect any movement, any rustle of a leaf. And fifteen thousand Englishmen looked toward the fort. Not only these. There were also the eyes of the Huron, the Mohawk, and the Rangers.

All they saw, floating toward the outlet of LaChute, was a small green hemlock. They did not see the head that bobbed along inside it. And the blue eyes of Fawn Charbon did not see them, until he reached the soggy marshland on the south bank below the fort. There sat a squad of French soldiers armed with muskets, to guard the southern waterfront where the tiny French colony had built its village of huts and cabins.

The hemlock floated away, into the quiet waters of Lake Champlain. Only Fawn's nose popped up, his face covered with a mantle of green slime. Old Foot had called it frogspit. Even with his ears below the water, Fawn could hear the soldiers talking. High to his left was the gray wall of stone, the south wall.

Underneath, he swam upstream, seeking until he found what he sought, the drainage ditch from the meadow west of the fort. Its water was only ankle-deep, but the ditch was low. Slowly, he moved up the muddy trench to the high ground. No one would recognize him now, he thought, as the son of Henri Charbon. He would only be a target, a mud-covered Mohawk.

Fawn thought he knew where the ditch would lead. In it, he crawled north. But the ditch ended in a thick twisted darkness of fallen trees. To go east was impossible, as the trunks of the trees became large and closely packed. To the west, the branches were opened. And when Fawn saw the first point of a limb, a yellow point that shot out from the black bark that had been made by an axe, he knew where he was. Far west of the fort, and in the worst possible place.

The sun, from what little he could see of it, was high in the sky. Now he must work his way back to the ditch, or discover a gap in the logs.

The bagpipes began once more. A lonely piper started his tune and the whole swarm took up the chant. Only this time they were close, very close, and coming closer. Fawn retreated deep inside the tangle of fallen trees, for now that he could see the advancing Redcoats, it was his only shelter.

PUFF!

He heard the first musket discharge from somewhere above his head, at the base of the trees. A French finger pulled a trigger, impatient to hit one of the red coats. And then, like a storm of thunder, thousands of muskets unloaded against each other. There was a space between two massive trunks. Fawn backed into it feetfirst, so his eyes could see the advancing Highlanders.

Like red ants they came. From everywhere, out of the green forest wall, until all he could see was the limp curled leaves of the fallen trees and the red of British tunics. Line upon line of Black Watch poured from the shelter of the west wood, charging the gunfire and mortars of the French who fought above his head.

Fawn had heard thunder, the angry voice of the Sky

God bringing rain. But the Sky God was a chirp of the wren compared to the God of War, he thought. Several times his hands covered his ears as the cannon shook even the great trunks of the trees. He heard the screams of men in pain. The air was heavy with gunsmoke, and the stench of exploded sulphur and black powder stung his nose. His lungs filled with the fumes. Coughing and choking, he lost his morning meal deep inside the noise and the darkness of the fallen trees.

The battle continued. More of the men in red uniforms came. And more followed those. At first they stepped over their fallen comrades. But as the mounds of dead and dying Scotsmen rose higher, the advancing soldiers now climbed the hills of bodies, their boots kicking the still faces. Several waves of British advanced over the tops of the felled trees to within bayonet range of the French lines. Drops of warm red blood-slime dripped down through the timbers, hitting Fawn's back.

Again he retched, though his belly held no food.

No Mohawk, no Huron; he saw only thousands of men in thousands of red coats. Charge after charge. How, wondered Fawn, will so few Frenchmen repel such courage? There was no end to the ranks of the Black Watch. They came and they fought and they fell until the limbs of the big trees were woven with the limbs of fallen men.

Above his head, French cannon released round upon round of grapeshot. Then reloaded, touched off again until the French mortarmen who manned them screamed as they handled the burning iron. Yet the throats of the big guns continued to roar.

One company of Redcoats did reach the French lines; and above his head, Fawn heard the clatter of musket against musket. Bayonets into bodies. A British soldier fell backward, down among the thick wood. His arm was swinging, hanging lifeless in its red tunic less than an arrow length from Fawn's face.

Blood ran out from under the red sleeve, dripping on the wood until long after the arm was still. The hand bled white, and only then did its bleeding stop.

It appeared to Fawn (as he had lived close to a fortress and had seen many uniforms) that the man was an officer. There was braid on the red sleeve. Moments later, the officer's pouch slipped down from his shoulder. Fawn saw the name that had been tooled into the leather flap. "Col. Donaldson" would never return to the hills of Scotland.

More of the British came, and a few of the colonials. Fawn looked for Ben Arnold in the smoke and noise. But there was little to see now, except for a mountain of fallen bodies, the dead and dying that had once been the core of General Abercromby's force. It is hard to remember, Fawn said to himself, that this is the same British army that I saw only two days ago coming north in as many whaleboats as there are fish in the lake.

The sun retreated over the mountains to the west. There was little noise except the feeble whimpering of soldiers only half dead. A few muskets discharged here and there. But the Redcoats no longer attacked the French lines. The volley of cannon stopped and did not resume. The smell of dead men who rotted in the summer heat, and the sound of men who prayed to die filled the air as the wail of the bagpipes earlier had filled it. Only now the pipes no longer played. The British withdrew, leaving their dead. Leaving the dying to die alone.

The French had held, and won.

His father was safe. Fawn felt that the British would not return for another swallow of such a bitter loss. Somewhere a French soldier shouted. Other soldiers took up the cry, remembering the quiet patrician general who had made them sweat for a day and a half cutting trees until they could no longer lift an axe, the man who had planned the defense of Fort Carillon. And the shouts of tribute became a chant.

"Montcalm! Montcalm! Montcalm!"

There were other yells of "long live France," but the name of their noble commandant rang out again and again, in a united barrage from the mouths of his battered but unbeaten men.

"Montcalm! Montcalm!"

The general would live, perhaps happily skip another flat little pebble on the sunny surface of the lake-waters.

"Montcalm!"

Fifteen

Fawn waited for night to come.

Wedged between the giant trees that lay piled like firewood, his body was stiff and his belly was empty. But he knew he could neither sleep nor eat. In his chest, his heart still pounded with the beat of battle. His eyes burned with the smart of gunpowder, and birds sang a long steady note in his ears. So this is war. This is how the French and the British meet, soldier against soldier. Who, Fawn wondered, decides that such a horror of a meeting will take place? Old men, he thought. Old fools who command young fools to die.

Years ago, Old Foot had told him of his early manhood, his raid of a Huron village far to the north. Many Huron had been killed. Fawn had asked Old Foot how many Mohawk had died. Old Foot did not answer. Had he lived, Old Foot would have sent his grandson to die against the French and the Huron. Fawn wondered, was Old Foot one of the old fools? With all his winters, did he not know there is more to life than death, to kill our enemies or kill ourselves? Kill, kill, kill. The stink of it entered Fawn's nose with every breath. All around him, dead soldiers emptied their bowels in the summer heat. And insects crawled upon eyes that lay open, looking up, but never to see the sky.

Several times he wanted to crawl out from between the logs, to leave this place of death. But he could not force himself to move; for in order to go, he must crawl and drag himself through a tangle of dead British, their red coats made even redder from blood. Closing his eyes did not help, as the smell of dying stabbed into his nostrils with the sharpness of a bayonet. Again and again, it made Fawn gag. His stomach retched and heaved.

Finally the sun backed off, over the purple hills to the west, and the shadows swallowed the day.

Fawn's body was shaking as he edged out from between the trunks of the fallen trees. Dead soldiers lay everywhere. In the early darkness, he walked on legs and hands and faces. Fingers were still holding fast to muskets, as if the dead men did not know that their war was over. Fawn had always hoped to own a gun. Now he could have had thousands, and yet he did not want even one.

"Mary."

The word made him freeze. Dead men do not talk. He knew one of the Scotsmen said it, but which one? He was only aware that his hands quickly covered his mouth, because he wanted so very much to scream.

"Mary!" The voice was nearby, and this time it spoke louder. Looking around from side to side, Fawn saw only the mounds of red tunics, but not one of them moved. When he felt the hand close upon his ankle, he wanted to cry out: for his father, for Old Foot, for anyone to help him set himself free from a dead hand.

The face looked up at him. The mouth was open, the two eyes were open. As the soldier tried again to speak, his mouth widened and closed, but made no sound. Around his leg, Fawn felt the man's grip tighten as if clinging to life.

"Mary," he whispered. "Mary is my . . . wife, in Scotland . . . tell her, tell her . . ."

The voice stopped, and the mouth no longer moved. But the hand did not release Fawn's leg. Finger by finger, Fawn tore away the soldier's grip. His hand on

the man's wrist told him that the heart had stopped
beating.

WHAM!

Before he even heard the shot that came from the
French lines behind him, Fawn felt the ball of lead
bury into the earth nearby. Someone else had heard
the dying man speak in English. Now, thought Fawn,
now, while the French soldier reloads his musket.
Leaving the dead man among the regiment of dead,
Fawn ran toward the wall of trees and into the dark
of the forest. His ankle still felt the grip of the man
who died calling for his Mary.

Ahead of him, he heard men laughing. Moving forward through a dense thicket he arrived at a place
just north of LaChute where he could see and yet not
be seen in the moonlight.

The two Huron warriors were drunk.

On a fallen log, they sat facing each other, astride
the trunk as if it were a giant horse. As Fawn watched
from behind a clump of ferns, one Huron fell off the
log. The other warrior held a Black Watch bagpipe
and was trying to play it. His cheeks puffed out as he
partly filled the bag. A few squawks came forth,
which to Fawn's ear made poor music.

The man on the ground lay on his back, kicking both
his feet into the air. He wore only one moccasin. He was
singing a tune that was a mixture of both Huron and
French words, about a woman who knew many men.
He got to his knees and drank from an earthenware jug,
holding it high over his head. Fawn smelled the foul
smell of rum as the liquor splashed from the jug into the
man's face. Running down his chin and neck, the
spilled rum shined his chest. The warrior with the bagpipe grunted at him in Huron, making a sign to have
him put the corncob stopper back in the mouth of the
jug. The other man instead put the cob into his own
mouth, and tried to continue his song.

Fools, though Fawn.

Are they so sick with rum that they think it was the Huron who fought back the Redcoats? Yet better to die with rum than to die in war. Have these two Huron seen this day what I have seen? If they have, then can they be blamed for washing their memories with rum until the eye cannot see and the mind no longer remember? Suddenly, Fawn thought, I wish to drink rum, and to swallow it down my sickened gullet until the illness of this day is replaced by another illness. To burn my throat with rum until this battle is no more than a drunkard's dream.

So this is why men drink, to fill an emptiness that cannot be filled with rum, and yet they try. My father drank rum only for the cold, until the death of my mother. She was the cause then. And now, it is his son whom he thinks he has lost, as he has lost his robe of black, his carpenter, his beloved France. Perhaps when his mind swims in rum, all that he has lost returns to him, one by one to cherish, to comfort him in his lonely darkness. He drinks so that what he dreams appears real, and what is real is only a dream.

The one warrior continued to blow into the bagpipe, faster and faster, but produced little tune. It appeared to Fawn that the bag had a hole in it, which the Huron did not see. His eyes were too dim with rum. Did the two Huron fools believe that the British would never return to dislodge Montcalm from Fort Carillon?

As Fawn watched the two drunken men, a third Huron came from behind the trees. Except for a red Scottish cape around his loins, he was naked. As one of the warriors was again about to swallow rum, the third man (who seemed to be a chief) kicked the jug from his hands. Hitting a rock, the rum jug shattered. Yet it was not a kick of rage but of disgust. He dropped his cape over the log.

The man with the bagpipe tried to explain, but the chief commanded his silence. Calmly taking the bagpipe from his hands, he threw it to the ground and spat upon it. The man who had held the bagpipe jumped up from the log and hurried away through the trees. The man who had done the singing tried to rise from the ground, but instead only staggered and fell.

The chief's hand rested on the handle of his knife. He carried no bow, no arrows; only the long knife that rode his right hip as though it had sprouted from the bone. Swelling his chest and slowly breathing out one deep breath, the chief bent low over the fallen warrior. With a quick upward motion, he swung the helpless man over his shoulder as if he carried a dead deer. Then scooping up his red cape from the log, he melted into the trees with his burden.

Alone again, Fawn looked around in an effort to spy a familiar rock or tree. Nothing looked as he had seen it before. The woods were torn by an army that had advanced and then retreated. Time after time, as he moved through the trees toward the sound of La-Chute, his foot kicked some item or other of military gear that had been hurriedly left behind by the retreating French.

Here was a drum, there a tin of gunpowder.

Reaching the waterfall, Fawn knew at last where he was. Waiting until the moon was covered by a cloud, Fawn followed the creek at the top of the falls, heading toward the small longhouse where he lived with his father.

Only the house was not there.

Fawn found only a pile of tree bark and broken poles. Even the cooking pot was smashed. As the wind rips an old birdnest from a tree, so had their home been torn from the land. Nothing remained but a heap of useless rubble. As he stood there, he felt as though something more than a little hut had come to an end. They could not kill the fort of General Montcalm, he thought, and so their rage kills the tiny fort of Henri Charbon and his son.

Looking up into the moonlight, Fawn whispered "Old Foot, do not look down and see what I see, as it will make your heart heavy with sorrow. And bitter with revenge. Do not burn, Old Foot. Your life that follows the life is not to be filled with regret. You hunted well, your bow was strong and your arrow true, so do not sing sad songs. Dance around the fires in the sky with new feet that are fleet and young, along trails from star to star that have no sharp rocks to pierce your moccasins. And one day, Old Foot, your Fawn will join you and together we will stalk a deer that hides behind the moon."

Having finished his prayer, Fawn dropped to his knees and began to dig into the dirt under the bark floor with his hands. Not finding what he sought, he dug again in another nearby place and then another and another until at last his fingernails scraped against the small bundle of deerskin. Working carefully so as not to damage the contents, he finally burrowed beneath all four edges and lifted the small parcel of deerhide from the hole in which it had been buried. With care, he gently brushed the moist specks of dirt from the folded deerskin. I am thankful, he thought, that whatever tore down our home did not dig beneath our floor to find what I buried.

He felt the deerskin, pleased that only the outer layer was damp. Inside, the layers were dry, which meant the contents of the bundle would too be dry. This is good, Fawn thought.

The wind came, and suddenly Fawn was cold. He wanted a fire. But now there was no hut that would hide the light of flames. If only he had a blanket. His hand touched the bundle, and he thought for a moment of unwrapping it to use the deerskin to sleep in. No, he then thought. No. What was in the folds of deerhide must be cared for.

Huddled in the darkness, holding what he had unearthed close to his chest with both arms, Fawn tried to sleep with his back to a tree. But sleep would not come. He thought of his supper with Ben. Only a day ago, yet so much had happened in a single day. So much war and so very much death. He found himself wishing Ben were here, to share a rabbit and to talk. Together they would build a fire, so that one could watch and the other sleep.

At last his eyes closed, and sleep came to comfort him and to bathe his body with rest.

How long had he slept? Fawn was quickly awake, suddenly listening for a noise when there was no noise. Old Foot had said that danger is always silent as it walks the night on padded feet. Now, why was he listening to the stillness and the distant tumbling of LaChute? Was it only the wind that moved through the trees? Then he heard the sound that had opened his eyes. The crunch of a foot upon twigs, a careless foot. No animal would walk so. Animals are too wise. Even the great bear steps only on shadows.

Fawn did not move, except to whip his eyes from side to side to see the unseen. It came again, the snap of brittle wood. Feet were running, shuffling through the carpet of pine needles behind his back. How many feet? Hard to tell, but perhaps only two.

Large clouds blanketed the moon, and there was little light for Fawn to see. He rolled quickly to his stomach, an arrow in his bow. Drawing back the cord, he did not stop until the wings of the arrowhead almost reached his left hand. It was the same arrow that had killed the forkhorn. Now it must kill again. The arrow must see in the dark, as Old Foot had said, and fly like the furry bat, the fox that flies.

The footsteps came again, closer now. Closer, closer, nearer and nearer, until Fawn no longer heard the distant waterfall and was deaf to the wind that danced in the leaves. He heard only the rustle of pine quills as they themselves felt the weight of moccasins. His left arm was rigid, but it had started to cramp. Yet he dared not loosen his bow. Closer . . . closer . . .

Then he saw.

Sixteen

"Father!"

"Yes, yes, it's you, Fawn."

"They were both speaking French, as they often did. But only Fawn was aware that they spoke too loudly. Darkness has few throats but many ears.

"We must be still, Father," said Fawn, placing his hand gently over his father's lips. Henri Charbon nodded his head, and his son lowered his hand.

"Our home." Henri looked around, as if not knowing where to look. "Our house is not here?"

"No, Father," Fawn whispered, as the older man had also whispered, his lips close to Henri's ear.

"Where is it? Where?"

"Someone tore it down. Perhaps we should be grateful for the darkness, so that we do not see how little of it stands."

"But who? Why?"

"Be honored, Father. The British came north not to attack the stronghold of General Montcalm, but to destroy the lodge of an even greater soldier, Henri Charbon."

As he spoke, Fawn hoped that his father would respond to his words with a smile. The smile came, but went quickly.

"It was our home," said Henri, "our home."

"Until the fort was built. Then we were made to feel like a bothersome night bug about to be swatted. But now is not the time to seek pity. We both live, Father. Is that not enough?"

Suddenly, in that moment, Henri Charbon felt that he did not talk to a boy. Fawn seemed to be in charge of their condition and not he. Everything that Henri could think of to say sounded like a question that a child asks of a parent. What will we do? Where will we go? How are we going to survive? He thought, I am nothing but a frightened and foolish old man.

"Look there," he said, "it's starting to get light."

"Morning comes."

"Perhaps now," said Henri, "we can survey the damage and repair it."

"Father, there is little to repair. Take comfort in the fact that we ourselves were not inside asleep when whoever it was discovered our house."

"Yes, we must be grateful. I am most thankful that my son is alive and well. Where were you during the battle?"

"Far away," said Fawn.

"It was dreadful. I saw the whole of it from the fort wall. How our boys ever held that onslaught of British was a miracle. The air was so heavy with gunsmoke, it was difficult to see much. Our boys had courage."

"So did theirs. Scotsmen do not die as cowards."

"Then you saw?" said Henri.

"A small part, yes. When a battle is so large, no man could say he saw it all."

"We sent out scouts to follow their retreat. One returned to tell us that the British have withdrawn to their camp on the upper lake. Do you think they will again attack?"

"Yes, but not soon. Another army of Redcoats will come, perhaps even a larger one. Or even a smaller force under a more able chief."

"We killed one of their generals. I heard so at the fort. Two days before the battle. It was about the time you came home carrying your deer. One of our scouting patrols ambushed a small advance of Englishmen and killed one of their top officers."

"Lord Howe, their brigadier. He was also the grandson of the first George of England."

Henri Charbon looked at his son in disbelief. How could he know such things? Unless, unless . . . no, he could not think such a thought. Did my own son join an English army to fight against the flag of France? My own son? The pain in my heart is real, Henri thought. God, what a hurt. But I cannot think this thing. Yet when Old Foot was wounded and then died slowly of his wound, I knew Fawn wanted revenge upon the French.

"So you sided with the British?" said Henri.

"Fawn Charbon sides with no one. It is not my war. And the Huron, the Mohawk, both are fools to fight for a victory that never will be theirs. Not as long as there is a white face to claim it for himself, and a white hand to wave a flag. Fawn holds no love in his heart for France, a land whose deer I will never hunt. But I do not scatter my arrows against French cannon to please the Yengeese and to wear a red coat as do some of the Mohawk. Nor do I wear the small face of George the White Father around my neck like a collar on a dog. Fawn is not Old Foot. I believe that a British medal around the neck of a Mohawk is like the snare that loops a rabbit's neck, only to break it. Whether it cuts off the air or cuts off the land, the difference is small."

"Then how . . . ?"

"How do I learn of the death of Lord Howe? A friend told me," said Fawn.

"A *friend*?"

"Yes. Is it so strange, Father, for your son to have a friend?"

"Fawn, Fawn . . . you misjudged me. If any boy ever *needed* a friend, it was you."

"Need? A joke, that word. Fawn Charbon *needs* his life and nothing more. I have my bow, my father, and one friend. But he is a friend I *want*, yet do not need."

"Your friend is a Mohawk?"

"No."

"Not a Huron?"

Henri Charbon saw his son spit on the ground. A foolish question. No grandson of Old Foot would befriend the Huron.

"A Scotsman?"

"No, Father, not a Scotsman. And our wits are dull to stay here and let our words betray us."

Together they moved silently through the trees, Fawn in the lead carrying the bundle wrapped in deerskin; his father followed. Where, thought Henri, do we go? He stopped and held onto a tree.

"No, Fawn. I am weak from no sleep, and I cannot travel."

"Why then did you leave the fort?"

"To look for you."

It was almost morning now, and Henri Charbon could read the look of patience on his son's face. I wish him to know so much, Henri thought, that even though my arms no longer rock him to sleep in the dark of a winter night, my heart will hold him forever.

"You are brave," Fawn said. "But you also think me a fool."

"Foolish, yet not a fool. Can any man who walks say that he has always been a fox? General Abercromby was a fool, yes. And your General Montcalm is foolish if he believes the British are so battered that their boats will never again come north. More than that, you and I are fools to care."

Henri Charbon sat upon the wet earth of morning. His eyes wanted to close and rest. Instead they looked at his son, who seemed so much taller now.

"That object you hold, what is it?" said Henri.

"Sometimes the things we least require are what we long for," said Fawn.

The boy was looking down at him, smiling. He is beautiful, Henri thought. Blue Voice had a face that was soft and fair, and our son is a sweet echo of her beauty. He is a wild flower. His face is the face of

Blue Voice, and when he smiles at me as he now smiles . . . oh, Fawn . . . you will never know and I shall never tell you. For even if your smile is your mother's, your spirit is Old Foot. Wild flower pretty and wild flower strong.

Then he remembered what Fawn had said about the death of Lord Howe. Had his own son gone to the enemy camp and offered information of Montcalm's position and strength? Was that how he made a friend, tattling to the hungry ear of some bagpipe-blowing devil . . . or worse, some naked Iroquois whose highest aspiration in life was to tear flesh from the bone of Jesuits. Wild flower, I call him. Wild animal!

"Father, we cannot stay here. Years ago you and Old Foot made the house when there was no Fort Carillon to foul our land. So now the time is come for us to swim like a fish or fly like a bird, to be part of the fort or to leave this place. We must choose, for now we live between two beehives and yet we are not members of either swarm."

How bright he is, Henri thought. Like a newly minted coin; and his voice has the ring of copper, with words of worth. His face may be Blue Voice, his spirit may be Old Foot, but his mind is mine. He is a scholar, by damn! Better still, a thinker. I find myself resenting his outbursts, yet I must bow to his reason and logic. How old Brother Anthony would have inspired Fawn. How rapturously my old teacher would have prized such a pupil.

"Why do you smile at me, Fawn?"

"Because I feel joy."

"Joy?"

"Yes. I know that what I hold in my arms will please you, Father."

"I am confused. Is it food? *Rum*?"

"To you, it is more than both."

His son knelt upon the leaves, and slowly (as if he wished to delay his moment of surprise) unfolded the dirt-covered wrapping of deerskin, layer by layer.

"Books!" said Henri.

"I buried them where they would be dry and safe, so they would not be destroyed."

"My books, my books."

"Remember this one?" said Fawn. His hands reached for the volume by Sir Francis Bacon, the brilliant Englishman. As if he held a young bird, he handed Henri the book.

"The one from Fort Saint Frédéric," said Henri, "the book I brought back with me through the snowstorm."

"We thought you were crazed," said Fawn, "to bring back a book. We thought the cold had snapped your mind."

"I was a fool."

"No, Father. It was Old Foot and Blue Voice and Fawn. We were the three fools . . . without rum, and without understanding."

"You can see that now? You can really understand why I trudged twenty miles through snow and cold with it?"

"Yes. For the same reason I hide my canoe, and carried home my first deer. A man must hold fast to his treasure."

"You are wise, Fawn."

"Like you, Father, I am perhaps both wise and foolish. Think of our laughter in this very place. Our summers and summers of laughter, not caring who heard."

"How we yelled in French to the Huron, and in English to the Mohawk," said Henri.

"And how my grandfather yelled in Mohawk to everyone," Fawn laughed. "Lucky for us his voice was old and brittle as a brown leaf, and yet his spirit was the white crust of winter."

"Good times," said Henri, looking at his son, "we had good times whenever we could."

"Until the fort was built."

Henri Charbon watched as his son turned his face

to look back, wondering what the boy was remembering. "Fawn, you always resented the building of Fort Carillon, didn't you?"

"Yes."

"Why?"

"Because this land was once ours, to fish, to hunt, to take joy in its seasons. I wish the British to return and reduce that fort to a pile of rock and burning timber."

"How can you say such things?"

"Because my heart says them, in Mohawk."

"Perhaps we should return to the fort," said Henri, thinking to himself that this is only a dream, "and perhaps you and I could become Frenchmen."

"Father, I wish for nothing more than to live as what I am. My eyes are sad to see how much *you* wish to be French, among French, and how little you ever became part of your tribe of Frenchmen. It was as if Old Foot had tried to join the Huron. Your tribe did not want you, Father."

"How can you hurt me so?"

"It was the French who hurt you. And if my mother had still lived, they would have hurt a Mohawk woman even more. As I remember the death of Old Foot, I can spit into French faces three times, for three reasons."

"They hurt you, too," said Henri, "the boys at the fort."

"No . . . as I have no feeling. The French have given me wisdom. I learn that each animal must stay with its own kind. The bear finds no shelter in the lair of the panther."

Seventeen

Henri Charbon sat on the ground, watching his son gently wrap the books once again inside the soft thickness of buckskin.

"I will carry them," said Henri. "After all, they are my books. Come."

"To what place?" said Fawn.

Henri was pleased. For a moment, he felt the leader and Fawn the follower. Do I really know what to do? Henri's mind was running, trying to think with enough speed to stay ahead of his son. Thinking of nothing to say, he bundled the books under one arm and started to walk, heading north, down the hill toward the big meadow that many French axes had cleared to give Fort Carillon a view north—as if the soldiers of Montcalm had sought a backward glance toward Canada, Henri thought. Canada and France and home. My God, he said to himself, looking north on Lake Champlain, as more and more of the blue water came into view. How I do want to go home. Not here, not Canada, but home to France.

"Home," he said aloud. The word almost caught in his throat. Home! What a lovely sound. "If I knew we were heading toward France, I could walk every step of the way."

"I believe you could, Father."

Henri looked at his son. "You know, when a man is a priest, there is no honor that can compare to hearing a pure young voice, a child, calling him Father. But with you, Fawn, the honor I hold dear is that I truly *am* yours."

Glancing at Fawn as they walked, he hoped to see a glimpse of warmth on the lad's face. Perhaps he should be thankful the boy heard his words and not wish that he also shared his feelings. He sighed, noticing that Fawn's face wore no expression. He will be a man of secret thoughts.

"So often I wonder," he said, "why I cannot be father enough for you. Ironic. As a child in France, I was never boy enough to please my father. Perhaps not man enough to 'please my wife. I guess you learned far more from Old Foot than from me."

"Many things," said Fawn, "but not all things. When we learn to swim, do we watch a hawk? Or to run, do we chase a turtle? How strong would Old Foot be in the forests of France? Would he stand among Frenchmen as you stood among the Mohawk? Old Foot was brave, but no stouter than you."

"Fawn, you startle me always with your philosophy, and your understanding. I was educated to believe that wisdom comes from books."

"I have heard the words you read from your books, and some are brittle words that would snap in an icy wind."

"An icy wind," Henri said. "The thought of one more winter in this place . . ."

"Then go," said Fawn. "Find your place in France, where the sun is always warm to ripen the grapes and where the ground is never hard."

"Home to France?"

"Yes, home to France."

It was as though Henri had swallowed some strange tincture of medicine prepared by a weird hag to conjure up the sweet agonies of memory. "I am homesick, Fawn. So ill for the sight and smell of France that I suffer in my breast. I wish so much to go home. I wish to return to the church. Would you come to France with me so that I may shout to the world that

you are my boy? Even the Holy Father in Rome I
would tell, and with pride."

"Rome," said Fawn. "The place in Italy that people
built on seven hills."

"There! You see, you know Europe already."

"I know only Fawn Charbon."

"Yes, my son. I believe you have the unique gift of
knowing yourself. Three days ago, you were just a boy
who had slain his first deer. And you lugged it home,
as would any boy, to show his father and to share the
meat. But now you grow so manly."

"I have also found a friend, and killed an enemy."

"You *killed* a man?"

"Old Foot was wrong. My heart did not sing because I slew a Huron."

"You shall never know, Fawn, how *my* heart sings
to hear you say so. But tell me of your friend. What is
his name and where did you meet him?"

"He is called Ben Arnold. He was tied to a tree, yet
he kicked a Huron between the legs."

"Was the Huron about to kill Ben Arnold?"

"Yes."

"So you killed the Huron?" said Henri.

Fawn nodded to the question. Then he looked at
the earth, moving a small stone with the toe of his
moc. "Old Foot was wrong. It is not a happy thing to
spill the blood of other men. It is a sad thing."

"And if it were now," said Henri, "and you saw your
friend tied to a tree, would you again kill the Huron?"

"Yes," said Fawn. There was no delay in his answer.
His voice was strong. Watching the boy's face, Henri
knew he spoke the truth. The grandson of Old Foot
would kill, yet not for its joy.

"Is your friend Ben a British soldier?"

"No, he is one of the Yengeese who do not fight in
red coats. His name is Benedict Arnold from a place
called Connecticut. His father is a soldier, yet he
wants Ben to become a druggist."

"A druggist! And will he be?"

"Perhaps. Although I do not know what a druggist is or does. It has much to do with the bowels of old women and gunpowder. I think Ben Arnold will be many things."

"Fawn, can you ever understand why I again wish to be useful and to serve? To be a Black Robe?"

"No, for I do not know what Black Robes do. Except to make prayers for people, and to come to the land of the Mohawk where the Huron tremble like wet dogs. So now you have seen this land, this Ticonderoga of two lakes, go home to France."

"Why must you say this in such a cold voice?"

"Because I do not wish to close my eyes and see my father grow old and weak, only to beg at the door of a French fort for an edge of half-eaten bread. No man should die without a home."

Henri's eyes strayed from Fawn's face, looking over his shoulder and into the dark trees where they had cleared a hidden place for their longhouse. "Just over there," said Henri, "is a cave where I first heard your little cry. This is our home, where *you* were born. A home for all four of us to live, when there were four of us."

"And to die," said Fawn, "or to almost die during winter upon winter."

"Here we lived," said Henri, "and here we laughed. Here we buried our dead, and faced another winter."

"But in our strong years we were four, Father. And the winter was only one."

"Yes, only one. Against the four of us winter had no chance."

"We melted it each spring," Fawn laughed, "with our little fire."

"For me," said Henri, "that one little fire will never go out. It shall be our eternal ember."

"And for me," said Fawn. "But only trouble lives with us now, so that we fear to strike a fire. You must go home to France and be a priest."

"Never again a priest. A brother, perhaps."

"A brother then. But safe in France. Go home, Black Robe."

The name that Old Foot had given me, thought Henri . . . how much it brings to memory. Things to forget, and things always to cherish.

"What about you?"

"Fawn Charbon will go to Connecticut."

"I have seen maps at the fort, my boy, and Connecticut is many days from here."

"I am sixteen. I have many days and more. Do not bear the duty to build a nest for me, Father, for I am no longer a speckled egg. The nest I seek is where I am the father eagle."

"And so you fly to Connecticut to be an *Englishman?*" It was not easy for Henri to use the term.

"New England, New France. These are words, and our land may be bigger than that. Bigger than France or England or Italy, a great new tribe made from warriors of many tribes. Ben speaks of this, and there is iron in his voice. His heart is not soft for England. The British may learn this land is not so easily won."

"A lesson taught by Frenchmen," said Henri.

"I saw a dead Redcoat, his face buried in mud. From his back, a Huron arrow stood tall and straight as a tree, as if a Huron warrior had planted it there like a tiny flag. The arrow was proud. So proud that I was filled with sadness that I had sent another Huron to the clouds."

"And are you just as sad for the fallen Englishman?"

"No," said Fawn.

"Why not?"

"Because this is not his land. He came not to plant corn or gather hickory nuts. Instead he came to kill, but not to protect his den or his cubs. England is his home, just as France is yours. At first I thought, let the French come. They will not drive us away, as Old Foot said. But now there is no Old Foot to help defend us. Now the British and the Yengeese come, to go and then come again. You fought and I fought. We are two, and the soldiers are thousands. So take your books and go . . . Black Robe."

"Go, Black Robe," said Henri. "Do you know who said those words to me many years ago?"

"Yes. It was Old Foot. And now my ear hears his voice speak to his grandson. Go south, the voice whispers to Fawn, and learn new ways. Plant corn in new ground and share it with new faces."

"Is this the end of us? Is this all?"

"It will be if we stay. Go north, Black Robe. That is what I hear the spirit of Old Foot bark to the ear of his Jesuit friend. Go north to Canada and home to France."

"Home to France," said Henri. "If I could only go."

"You can. There are boats every moon or so that come south to the fort and return north. Go back then to the fort, await the boat, and leave. Return to your tribe."

Looking at his son, Henri knew he had never seen Fawn's face stare at him with such intensity. Was it affection or hatred, and would he ever know? And suddenly, he did know. The blue eyes were filling. Not in years had he seen his boy weep, for Old Foot would not allow it. And never had the voice of his son trembled. Perhaps it is best if he goes to Connecticut with his friend, and I go to France. Don't let me weep, God. Please don't let me weep. Fawn must not remember me as a wet-eyed old man.

"I will," said Henri. "And you must run to find your friend Ben, and plant corn in Connecticut. But remember our little house that was our home, and always and forever keep our little fire burning."

"Our little fire," Fawn's voice was as quiet as his mother's had been. "We were the first fort, Father. You and Mother and Old Foot and I are the real Carillon. The bells who first sang here. We are Ticonderoga."

"We are," said Henri, "then and evermore."

"Know this, Father. Old Foot was more than a grandfather to me. He was a teacher to honor, as you respected Brother Anthony. Old Foot was more than a toy of my youth."

Henri tried to speak but the words would not come. "I understand," he tried to say.

"But I am not the son of Old Foot. I am *your* son. I hunt as Fawn, son of Black Robe. I walk as Fawn Charbon, to carry not Old Foot's name, but yours."

"Behold my son," said Henri, "in whom I am well pleased."

"My boyhood was Old Foot. My manhood . . . is you."

Fawn was reaching out now, his Mohawk face coming closer. Henri felt the strong young arms around him, almost breaking his bones and his heart; holding him as if he, an old man, were nothing but a little child. The body against his body was tight and trembling. Against his face, Henri felt the wet young cheek. Go to hell, Old Foot. This is my boy. Do you hear, you old red Mohawk devil? *My* boy! And we shall both cry if we damn well please. You had him, Old Foot. But you have lost him, and I have found him, to know he is forever mine.

Fawn was running now, headed south across the open meadow where black-and-white cows once again were grazing, running toward the great gray star of Fort Carillon. Smaller and smaller he grew as he turned west and into the trees. Henri was hoping that Fawn would turn one last time and wave farewell, but he did not. He was out of sight and forever gone. Gone, thought Henri, gone. Old Foot, he said, once again you cut out my heart, but you no longer own my son. Nor do I. The land owns Fawn, and one day he shall own the land, to show no mercy on those who try to take it from him. Looking south toward the fort, Henri Charbon remembered a Bible phrase that Brother Anthony had quoted from the Book of Job:

"There is a path which no fowl knoweth, and which

the vulture's eye had not seen. The lion's whelps have not trodden it, nor the fierce lion passed by it."

If the Lion of England devours New France, thought Henri, let the Lion himself take heed.

Lion, he thought, beware your whelp.